PRAISE FOR APPALACHIAN MOUNTAIN MYSTERIES

"A real treat, highly recommended for its fine attention to both detail and the psyches of investigators who confront themselves as much as the threat at hand." ~**Midwest Book Review**

"This series by Lynda McDaniel is my favorite by far. The characters have such believable personalities that grab you and make you feel as if you are there with them. Nothing about these books is a turn off. The language is clean, the descriptions are so on point on that you can almost feel the breeze, smell the clean air and get totally lost in the words." ~**Lori J.**

"Human kindness ... the scenery is beautiful and the town folks are people I would like to meet." ~**L. Helton**

"Lynda McDaniel writes magical stories. She brings out the very best in her characters. As the reader you want Abit to find true happiness and you can't wait to get to the end to see what next lies ahead of him. You get the impression that you are right there with him." ~J. Davis

"Thoroughly enjoyable and intriguing with descriptive powers and beautiful mountain scenery. Intense family and friend dynamics with character vulnerabilities and complex relationships that steal the reader's heart and make this mystery a must-read." ~Pam Franklin, international bestselling author

"Excellent ... a breathtakingly beautiful series of human decency!" ~Amazon Customer

"Just like the people in your family, the characters in this series continue to grow...and grow on you. Each book in the series has been a joy to read. The storyline, the setting, and the hero make this book feel like you wouldn't mind living there and having Abit craft a one-of-a-kind bookcase for you. The drama and mystery just add to the fun!" ~Jude

"McDaniel's mystery novel delivers a pair of unforgettable crime-solving characters. I hope Della, Abit, and the gang will be back!" ~Virginia McCullough, award-winning author of *Amber Light*

FINDING BOOKS YOU LOVE
JUST GOT EASIER

SPELLBOUND MYSTERY MAGAZINE

Spotlight on one author each issue

Insider chat about what we're writing

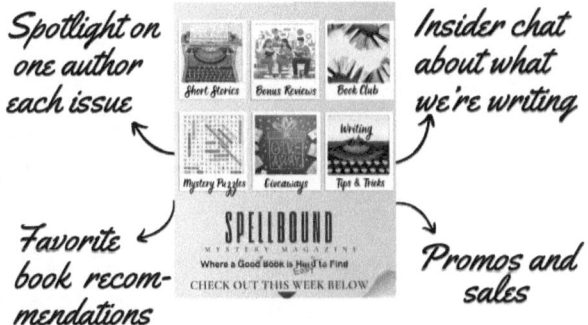

Favorite book recommendations

Promos and sales

MULTIPLE MYSTERY AUTHORS
IN EACH FREE ISSUE

SUBSCRIBE FOR FREE AT
HTTPS://SPELLBOUNDMYSTERYWRITERS.SUBSTACK.COM/

OR SUBSCRIBE BY CLICKING HERE

Up the Creek

A Mystery Novel

Lynda McDaniel

Published in 2022 by Lynda McDaniel Books.

ISBN: 978-1-7346371-7-5

Printed in the United States of America

Dedicated to Shug, the best friend anyone could hope to have.

Chapter 1
Abit

**Laurel Falls, N.C.
Summer 2009**

ALDER TREES KNOW NO shame. They sprout and grow and crowd out everything that gets in their way. Greedy for life. Like some people I've known.

Those trees were what brought me down to the creek that summer's day. I was sweating from all the sawing and swearing at the pretty little trees just because there were too many of them. I'd worked all morning, carving my way down a good piece of the creek.

By the time I'd stopped for a break, the sun had burned through the morning mist, though wispy patches still hovered, casting a ghostly glow. That was when I saw him. A man, lying crumpled in a place the trees had yet to claim. Half on the bank, half in the creek, his face dangerously close to the water. No sign he was breathing.

I hurried over and pulled him from the water and mud. When I stood again, my head swam, not from exertion but an overwhelming sense of sorrow. And the promise of more yet to come.

I sat a moment, the wet earth quickly soaking into my overalls. I studied the man as he lay there, silent-like. I'd been part of enough police matters to know I shouldn't move him any farther, but that creek was doing its best to suck the life right outta him. Something tugged at me to get him away from there—somewhere dry and warm. And safe.

He wasn't a big man, maybe five foot nine or ten, but dead weight felt twicet as heavy as regular. I ran to the house—up a slow rise and across a couple of acres—and got my wheelbarrow. I would've driven the truck, but it can't get down that far. (Well, it *can* get down that far; it just can't get back up). Besides, I'd never've been able to lift the man into its bed without doing him even more harm.

I bumped my way back down with the wheelbarrow, and as I approached the creek, I stopped short. He'd moved. Just a little, his arm now resting over his head. I let out a breath I hadn't realized I'd been holding.

"Listen, mister, this might hurt some, but do not be afraid." I soothed, as much for me as him. "I don't know where or why you were hurt, but I am here in good faith." Then I added, "And if you can hear me, I sure would appreciate any help in getting you into this wheelbarrow."

He didn't—couldn't—help, but somehow, by tipping the lip of the barrow down to the ground, I was able to ease him into its bed. He called out some gibberish, likely painful protests, when I tucked his legs into what they call the fetal position.

I pushed that wheelbarrow partway, then pulled it the rest of the way back up that slope. I had to stop three times to catch my breath, and each time I checked to make sure he still had his. I drove that cart with all my might and finally stopped in front of our chestnut log barn.

Half the barn was now my woodshop, and a few year ago I'd built a guestroom in the other half in what used to be cattle stalls. I wasn't that kind of farmer, so no need to worry about them losing their shelter. I had oncet thought about getting more animals than just chickens, but that promise had long ago faded. A number of friends and drifters had stayed in the guestroom, which was nice enough with the maple bedstead I'd made and a quilted coverlet—Bear Paw, I believe the pattern's called. I'd made a small kitchen and a pretty little table and chairs that sat under the window. I'd always enjoyed taking my meals looking outside, and I'd reckoned my guests would too. The window hosted a wooden flower box I'd built years ago, but now only black, bleak stalks remained, like stragglers at a funeral.

I pulled the coverlet offa the bed. No point in getting mud or worse all over it; the sheets would be easy enough to wash. The front door to the room was plenty wide—I'd used the frame that had guided those wide-hipped steers inside—so the wheelbarrow fit through just fine. Somehow, I picked that poor stranger up and settled him on the bed. I was never so happy to hear a groan.

"You're safe now, mister. I want you to know I am here to help you, not hurt you any further. Rest here for a while, and we'll sort things out later. I just hope and pray you won't be bringing any harm to my home. There's enough trouble going on already without you adding to it."

Though I'd just told him to rest, I knew I had to get those wet clothes offa him. Turned out he was harder to undress than my two boys, back when they were small and fell asleep on the way home from a concert or some other outing. I could tell his clothes were made of fine fabrics, even with all the muck and rank smell. A cut above anything from round here. I was able to pull off his soaking wet shoes, socks, and trousers easy enough, but his shirt was another story. I couldn't imagine what he was doing wearing such a fine, thin one—the kind men wear to offices and church—without a jacket. In these parts, he coulda frozen to death, even in the middle of summer. The shirt had stuck like glue, and as much as I hated to, I had to cut it offa him. I just couldn't budge him enough to do any different. I threw the tattered thing in a corner and pulled the sheet over him before rushing next door to my woodshop for a heater. After I plugged it in, I ran to the house for clothes.

I let the screen door slam as I hurried inside to see what I could find. I rummaged through my closet, but my six-foot-three frame called for clothing too big for him. I'd never had any extra weight, which gave me a leanness that registered as sharp angles and boney edges. As I closed the closet door, I caught a quick glance in the mirror. It surprised me to see how I'd grown even thinner than usual. Maybe that was why people, the few folks I'd been round lately, asked me if I was all right.

I sat on my bed and thought about the man. He was a complete stranger to me; I didn't have a clue what his story might be. My mind went to work on the worst things that could happen, like him getting better and trying to overtake me. I got so into it, I actually started to scare myself. Then my thoughts shifted to wondering if he was someone good—even great—who needed my help. That didn't last long. I was soon back to picturing him a ruthless killer.

I hated thinking thataway, but out here in the mountains, away from even the small town of Laurel Falls, I had to consider all the possibilities. And yet didn't that include good things happening too? I wondered what in my makeup kept me from seeing him getting well and offering me treasure instead of slitting my throat. Of course, I knew why. Good things like that didn't happen.

But for now, he was at death's door, and my only concern was keeping him from crossing over. Life is a fragile thing; it can change faster than the weather come March. So the way I saw it, we needed to throw our arms round what we had any given day. And what I had today was a stranger in my guest room, struggling to live.

Long ago, almost twenty year now, I'd made my own religion with kindness at its center. Kindness is mentioned more in the Bible than all the sins and misgivings Mama used to bring up on a daily basis. I'd come to understand the call to kindness when I was on a trip to Mt. Rogers park up in Virginia. I believe Jesus was there that day when wild ponies showed me about living life as each of us are meant to, natural-like. Not Mama's idea of what that life should be for me, certainly not Daddy's. Mine. That revelation gave me such a sense of peace and good will that kindness became my watchword. Lately, the way I'd been living here on the farm, I hadn't given myself much chance to show kindness, and it felt good to feel its warmth again.

Over the years I'd tried—and failed more times than I cared to remember—to show more kindness than the day before. But when you think about it, that's not such an easy task, especially when you take the time to explore the depths of kindness. Oh sure, it's easy to be kind when you're baking a birthday cake for your boy or helping a friend like Della Kincaid move heavy boxes at Coburn's General Store. Or coming to the aid of that stranger, so vulnerable at the moment. But what about harder acts of kindness, like calling an ambulance for him? I'd ignored that idea when it came to mind earlier, not wanting town folk roaming round my place. So who was I being kind to? Likely me more than him. And thinking ahead, was it kind to my boys to have a stranger living amongst us, someone who, for all I knew, could do us harm? My head ached with possibilities. By the time I'd finished arguing with myself, the sun had left that side of the house and the room began to feel cold.

I made myself get up and move to my boys' room. Not long ago I'd bought a few things on sale they'd need to grow into. At 12 year old, Vern was already taller and wider than Conor, even though he was a year younger. I figured his things would have to do. I also grabbed an old quilt we kept in the linen closet.

Back in the guestroom, I could tell the man hadn't moved. He did grumble as I gently placed the quilt over him. I saw a terrible mess on the pillowcase from a seeping wound I'd missed because of his tangled hair and all that creek water, washing it clear at the time. I kept a first aid kit in my woodshop (I needed it more often than I cared to admit); I brought that over and dressed his wound best I could, both for his sake and so I didn't have to look at its gore. I was able to stuff him into the sweatsuit and thick socks and then wrap him in the quilt, tighter than a newborn coming home from the hospital.

Throughout the rest of the day, I kept watch. Sometimes I'd tiptoe in and stand next to his bed, making sure he was breathing. Other times I'd stand by the door, just listening, not wanting to disturb him.

I couldn't help but smile, recalling the time I had the flu real bad, and the boys, back when they were just 8 and 9 year old, would come creeping into the bedroom to make sure their daddy wasn't dead. The first coupla times they did that, I was sick enough I couldn't say anything to assure them that, in time, I would be okay. But as I got better, I had to work hard at not laughing at their little faces, creased with concern, peering down at me. Finally I couldn't hold back, and I started to laugh. They jumped on the bed, and we rolled round together, happy I was back with them. I cherished that memory, especially now.

Oncet the busy work of survival was done, I didn't know what else to do. I started thinking about that ambulance again, but it didn't seem right not to give him a say. No telling what his story was and how he got into this state. Round here, we're careful about things like that.

He came to a coupla hours later.

Chapter 2
Abit

AT FIRST HIS SOUNDS didn't make much sense, just mumbles and sputters when he'd open his eyes wide and try to take in his surroundings. Eventually he adjusted some to his new situation, though he still stared at me with a big-eyed look. He musta seen nothing but trouble.

The room had gotten awful warm, what with the heater on and it being summertime. He tried to throw back the covers, but I had him so cocooned, he was trapped. That scared him too. When I pulled the quilt off, he looked down at his strange clothes, back at me, and back at his clothing. A wild fury filled his eyes. He tried to get up, but he wasn't going anywhere.

I worked at soothing him, telling him he was okay; he just needed to rest. He wasn't having any of that. His arms were flailing round, but there wasn't much he could do, not in his condition.

"Now listen, mister, no harm will come to you here. From the looks of that wound on the back of your head, you've already had plenty of that. I can call an ambulance right now and ..."

"No. No police. No," he growled.

We sat in silence for a spell. He stared at me with those crazy eyes, and my skin started to crawl. Finally I stood.

"I'm going to the house. I'm nearabout starved. I've got some soup I can warm for you, if you feel like eating." He shook his head. "Okay, but you've got to get your strength up." I wasn't sure where that came from; just something I'd heard Mama say at times like this. I left when he turned his head toward the wall.

Mollie came bounding over as I made my way to the house. In all the fuss, I hadn't wondered what had become of her. Just seeing her made my heart ease up a bit. She was medium-sized, covered in a shaggy coat that gave her the face of a movie-star dog. Not a day went by I didn't think how pretty she was. I had no idea where she'd been, but her paws were muddier than usual. She musta wandered off while I was cutting the alders and come back to the creek, where she'd smelled misfortune all the way to the house.

As we walked toward the porch, she stopped and started sniffing the air. She knew something was different, but didn't growl or carry on. I wished I could say that was a sign the stranger was a good man, but she was a silent dog. When she first came to live with us, I had the vet check to make sure she had vocal chords. One of the few people I could recall her growling at was that crazy serial killer I helped the FBI find. (That still sounds to me like something I made up.) Or that Johnny Ray Meeks, who crept round the barn, looking for my friend Nigel Steadman and trailing nothing but trouble. She had way more sense about things like that, and I'd grown to trust her. But for the most part, she liked everyone.

I bent down and patted her head. "It's okay, girl. At least I think it will be. He'll be here only a day or two, one way or another." She turned to go sniffing round the barn. I watched for a moment. When I didn't see her getting up to no good, I made my way to the house.

I warmed up the soup I'd made the night before—mostly pinto beans with vegetables from the garden and a little chicken. Tasted better this time round. I ate mine, then fixed a bowl for the stranger, though I didn't pack any cornbread for him. Too dry. It nearabout choked me, and he didn't need anything else threatening his life.

Back at the barn, Mollie was sitting quiet-like outside the guestroom, like a sentinel. For me or for him? Didn't know yet. I knocked on the door, and he grunted something I took for "Come in." I set the bowl on the table and turned to him. "I can help you eat this soup. You look like you need something; no telling how long you've gone since your last meal."

This time he nodded. I pulled the table close and fed him spoonsful at a slow but steady pace. I had to wipe his chin a time or two, the way you do a baby. I knew it must have felt awful to be in such a low place, but he just lay there, not registering much of anything.

When he'd finished the soup, some color had come back into his face. He nodded his thanks and kinda croaked, "Where am I?"

I gave him a quick rundown about the mountains and my farm. He looked confused, but who wouldn't be? Then he asked, "What's your name?"

"Abit Bradshaw." His eyebrows went up a little. "Long story," I added. I wasn't in the mood to tell him how I came by my first name. A mean old daddy who thought I was "a bit slow." I was, in some ways, but over time I'd learned how to live a regular life. Maybe a better life. But by then, the name had stuck. I coulda changed it, and I tried oncet using my initials, but that never caught on. Abit was what people'd always called me, and I no longer felt its taint. "What's yours?" I asked.

He looked terrified for a moment, then shrugged.

"Aw, come on, no need to be ashamed. If I shared my crazy name, you don't have anything to worry about."

"No, I don't know. I've been lying here with no idea where I am, who I am, or where I came from."

"That's likely from the nasty bump on your head. Give it a day or two, and your memory will come rushing back." Like I knew what I was talking about. "You're welcome to stay until then."

THREE DAYS WENT BY, one the same as the next. He was no trouble—that would come later. By the fourth day, when I knocked and went into the guestroom, I had to work at not laughing. He'd made his way outta bed, standing there in Vern's sweatsuit, its hem stopping a good two inches above the top of his socks. I recalled my own high-water-pants days and shared his embarrassment. He wore the oncet-fine leather lace-ups he'd arrived in; they were ruined for everyday wear, but good enough for now.

He solved my quandary by laughing at himself. "There's not a mirror in here, but I know I look ludicrous."

I let myself chuckle a little. Hard not to. I told him I'd gotten pretty good with needle and thread, and I could at least let the hem out. The shirt fit him fine. "You can wear some of my t-shirts for sleeping in," I added.

"Oh, I sleep in the nude."

I could feel the blood rush to my face. "Well, it would be nice if your memory came back on more useful information," was all I said.

He came over and stuck out his hand, like for a handshake. "I'm grateful for the clothing—and the care."

I nodded and shook his hand; I could tell he was getting his strength back. His grip felt strong, though his hand was as soft as a baby's. When I'd changed his head dressing earlier, the wound appeared to be healing proper-like. But still no sign of his memory. Every time I'd say we needed to go to the doctor, he'd get all panicky and say, "No police!" I hadn't even mentioned cops, though I reckoned he knew doctors and hospitals were supposed to call the authorities when something suspicious came their way.

I took a deep breath. "Well, I don't know what you could do round here."

"I would imagine in a day or two I'll be in good enough shape to leave. You could just take me to the nearest bus station."

"And do what?"

"Let me live the life of a drifter. I could take a bus to Wyoming and start over."

"And where is the money for this long bus ride coming from? You showed up here with no wallet, no ID. I'm not even sure you can buy a ticket without some kinda ID."

"I could work around your farm for a few days?"

"If your strength comes back. But what are you good at? You don't even know. Those hands of yours haven't seen a day of hard labor, at least in a long time. I'm just not sure how much help you'd be."

"You mentioned you're a woodworker. Even an idiot can sand."

I laughed. "And I'm just idiot enough to give you a try." I didn't bother mentioning there was more to sanding than he might've thought. "And you can help out with the chickens," I added. I was glad we had our brood, but with the boys away, they were just one more chore for me.

Looking round the room, he asked, "This guestroom, did you do it yourself?"

I nodded. I could tell he meant it as a compliment. That won me over. "Well, I'm sure I can find enough chores for you to earn your keep. I've let things run down a bit."

A heavy silence fell upon us after that. Unasked questions from both of us filled the room. Finally he cleared his throat. "Why are you taking such good care of me?"

I wasn't sure. I figured I felt sorry for him. I knew what it was like to be lost in your own skin. While over time I'd earned some relief from that lifelong weight on my soul, that feeling had become all too familiar again during the past year. What I said was, "Well, I've thought about that too. I reckon there's no need to make it more complicated than it is: You're a fellow man in need. You don't just turn your back on someone like that. And I know what it's like not knowing who you are."

He nodded, thinking that through. "But you don't know a thing about me. *I* don't know a thing about me. And what about your family? Don't you need to consult with your wife before I stay any longer? I've been looking out the window—I even stepped out in the yard yesterday when you were working. I can see signs of a woman around your farm. You must have a wife to go along with those boys you keep mentioning a hundred times a day."

He said that all with kindness, but it still raised my hackles. "Why *must* I?"

"I don't know. You seem like someone who's known love."

"Yeah, *known*. Past tense. She left."

Chapter 3
Abit

I COULD'VE SAID FIONA left *me*, but she swore she was leaving the *farm* set way out here in Hanging Dog. And missing what she loved: art and culture, teashops and things finer than I could give her. It was a long time coming, but eventually these hills closed in on her 'til she had trouble breathing. I'd known our days together were short when she started waking in the night, gasping for air. She was the nurse in the family, but even I knew she didn't have a medical condition.

It all started to unravel when we got back from Ireland that time the whole family went. Three weeks in Dublin thrilled her, even more than the trips back to Clifden where she was reared. She chattered on about the museums and cafes and shops. When we returned home, she seemed less of herself. Less bright. Less funny. Until.

What I didn't tell him was Fiona'd left without a word. I came home from delivering a bedroom suite, and she was gone. It was her day off from the hospital, and at first I thought she'd just run out to do something fun. I guess she had.

One thing I couldn't forgive her for is she used the boys to tell me she wasn't coming back. She'd talked with them when she picked them up from school, told them she was leaving. She dropped them off and sped back down the driveway. They came running to my woodshop, not crying yet. Shock still had its hold on them.

After they got over missing her so bad (it took weeks for that early pain to ease), we talked more about it. "Your mother hasn't been happy on the farm for some time," I told them.

"Yeah, and she loves us dearly, right? We know. She told us that," Conor said. Sarcasm was new to him. Vern just started to cry. I didn't have any wise words to share with them. We'd need to heal together, and that would take time.

At first I took it real personal-like. Who wouldn't? Even when Fiona kept saying it wasn't me but the place, I had trouble squaring that. Then she'd say she didn't hate me or anything like that, as if I'd been thinking thataway. I knew I'd never given her any reason to *hate* me, so I hadn't even considered it, at least not 'til she brought it up.

But truth be known, the last year with her had been hard. Like walking with a pebble in your boot, every step painful. You can still walk and do what you need to do, but all you can think about is the pain. And then when you finally stop and take the pebble out, the relief feels good. For a time.

Now all these months later, my heart was limping along okay, trying to catch up with what had already begun to make sense in my head: Fiona needed more from her life, and she deserved it.

I was grateful she didn't move to Dublin, but I knew she'd never put that much distance between her and the boys. She'd settled just an hour or so away in Asheville, for now. She went on and on about how she wouldn't take the boys away—not like what'd happened to Baldy, that poor tyke I'd gotten tangled up with in England. Said I'd given her the two things she loved most in the world. I didn't want to fight, but I did want to remind her those boys weren't just hers. Anyway, Conor and Vern were there now, visiting her in Asheville for a good part of the summer.

She'd made plenty of time for them throughout the past year. She'd pick them up from school before a weekend together and then drop them back home (with barely a wave in my direction). I'd offered to drive them down, but she said no. I reckoned she didn't want me to have any connection to her life down in the city.

Fiona wasn't the only one changed by that trip across the ocean. I came home from England different too. Lighter, shedding some of the sorrows that had weighed me down since I was a kid. The small-minded people I'd grown up with who'd tried to make me less? Their old taunts fell to the wayside. If I did hear them—from time to time, say, when I felt low—I wouldn't let them linger. That helped when she left. I'd hate to think how torn up I'd've been if I'd still carried all that shame.

But Fiona's leaving did throw me backwards. I took it pretty hard. And her discontent had grown so strong that it hung round like a haint, even in her absence. I pulled back from everything, except the boys. My woodworking partner, Shiloh, helped out a lot, moving into the guestroom and working side by side to get orders out. Back then I didn't care if I'd met those deadlines or not. Before, Shiloh and I'd always just tolerated one another—him acting all holier than thou with his Zen stuff, and me getting my back up when he did that. But I grew to understand that underneath his swagger, he was a good person. A gentle soul.

And then *he* left. He'd met a woman who, unlike the string of girlfriends he'd go out with for a month or two, stuck with him. Her daddy offered him some kinda job with his company, and they moved to Washington, D.C., of all places. With only a week's notice.

After that, especially when the boys were in Asheville, I did as little work as possible. I just hung round, drinking cheap beer and eating stuff right out of the fridge. I didn't care about much of anything, and the taint of failure I'd worked so hard to get rid of started to creep back in.

I'd just sit staring at the fire or watching the birds. I had a coupla feeders to attract the little ones; the bigger birds found their own food, swooping round the barn to catch insects and critters. Eventually I realized that even my birdwatching was lazy. I'd look at the pretty ones—the males with their bright reds and blues and occasional orange—and think the others all looked drab, dressed as they were in gray or brown. But with time, I could see that the females protected themselves and their babies with more muted tones, and the young'uns hung close to the adults, imitating them as they tried to figure out how to be in the world. Earlier I'd told myself the young birds weren't worth the effort of identifying since they'd be grown up before I could figure them out. Eventually, though, I began to appreciate how they were as special as their dressed-up daddy. You might say I learned about the young'uns while mine were gone. And that I needed to get my life together so my boys had someone worth imitating.

Chapter 4
Abit

"HEY, MR. BRADSHAW. GOT a postage due here for you."

Just that morning, the stranger had gotten all riled up, worrying about nosy visitors to my farm. I'd told him no one ever came this way, but then, sure enough our postman, Frankie Ivester, showed up. He usually left things in the mailbox at the end of the drive, but from time to time, someone shipped me something that needed money or a signature. As luck would have it, I was standing out in the garden, away from the barn and house, enjoying the sunshine after a coupla days of rainstorms. And who had just joined me but Alder? (That's the name I'd given him, in my own mind. I couldn't keep calling him the stranger; he wasn't even that anymore.) He had no way of getting to a good hiding place.

I felt an unease wash over me. Like guilt, but then I asked myself for what? Taking care of someone in need? No, it was more like fear—fear that Alder would become the grapevine topic of the week. I knew better than

to let my upset show, and Mollie helped out
when she ran over and started doing circles
round the postman, though he didn't seem to
mind. I reckoned he was used to that. Besides,
Mollie was just being friendly, not trying to take
a bite outta the seat of his pants.

I walked over Ivester's way, and he told me I
owed fifty cents. I dug out some coins, and my
hands kinda shook when I gave them to him. I
said thanks—but skipped any introductions. For
all Ivester knew, Alder coulda been a customer
or a drifter. He grunted something before
getting in his mail truck and heading down the
drive, but not before giving Alder a long stare.

"Oh crap!" Alder growled. "Do you think he
suspects something? And what about no one
coming here?" he asked, his tone sharp with
anger. He was kinda stomping round, and it
wouldn't be 'til later that week that I'd come to
understand why.

I ignored his second question. "Nothing to
suspect. You were just here, overseeing some
work I was doing for you." I believe I was trying
to convince myself as much as Alder.

"Dressed like this?"

"Well, I believe that's another clue."

"About what?"

"You're a snob. You came here dressed in fine
clothes with hands that hadn't done a decent
day's work in maybe forever. And now you're
making fun of the way we dress."

I was surprised when Alder chuckled. "I'm sorry about the hauteur." Then he quickly added, "I mean about sounding snooty. That doesn't really tell us much—other than possibly I've got more money than good sense." Then he turned real serious-like. "But I do know hoping people won't talk is naïve. That assumes a courtesy that no longer exits. Don't ask me how I know that, I just do. I hope your friends won't keep showing up unannounced."

I wasn't about to tell him I didn't really have any friends, at least not my own age. "Don't worry about them. They don't come here; we tend to meet up for a beer or a meal in town," I lied.

LATER THAT DAY, I realized I was glad Frankie Ivester had surprised us. Something about that visit shook me up, like a slap to the face that cut through the fog I'd been living in. I guess a jolt of fear can do that. I couldn't wait round for answers to land in my lap. I needed to figure out who in the world this stranger was—and what I was gonna do with rest of *my* life.

To that end, we started a regular practice of reading local papers. I already got the *Asheville Citizen-Times*, and I started a subscription to the *Watauga Democrat*. I also dug out old papers I'd stacked in the barn that dated back to a few days before I found Alder. Of a morning, we'd drink

coffee and read through them, looking for any
story that might ring some kinda bells with him.
We learned about plans for the county fair, a
suspicious fire at a U-Haul place, and our daily
horoscopes. (One told me to focus on the color
black more. I didn't hold with that. I'd been
trying to dig outta dark places, though maybe it
meant something different.) I also learned that a
Bill Monroe tribute band was coming to Boone,
and I thought I'd like to go to that. But nothing
that stirred any memories for Alder.

I couldn't afford the *Charlotte Observer*, so I
decided to visit the library over in Newland. We
were running low on groceries, and I could pick
up a few things while I was out. Before I left,
I told Alder not to answer the door if anyone
else came up the drive. He looked so worried I
took time to assure him that wasn't likely. "Don't
fret. Like I told you, no one comes to see me
anymore."

"That's what you said before the postal
carrier." I made a mental note about that—no
one round here said anything but postman,
even if it was a woman, so he was likely from
a town like Asheville or Charlotte. "And what if,
just say, someone *does* come? We need a plan for
how you will account for my presence."

"Just that you're my helper. Shiloh's gone. I
need you."

"Okay, but where did you find me? And what
about this big scab on my head?"

"Woodworkers are always getting bumps and scrapes. I walked into some rough-hewn slabs one time and nearly cut my leg off. At least that's how it felt. As for where you came from, I believe you'd set your sights on being a drifter not long ago. That's what I'll tell them. You're just doing odd chores for room and board before moving on." A sadness swept across his face. "I'm not rushing you. I've told you, you can stay as long as you need."

He looked at me real serious-like. "I still don't know why you're helping me so much."

I didn't want to get into that again. I just said, "Faith, I reckon. Everything comes down to faith. Crossing the street, eating food someone else made, driving a car. Without it, I can't imagine how we'd get through any given day."

WHEN I GOT BACK from the library (nothing of note in the *Observer*), we put up the groceries I'd bought in Newland, just enough to get by before I could make a big run. I was still waiting for a check for a sideboard I'd delivered almost two week ago. I also needed to get my nerve up to shop at Coburn's General Store without giving Alder away. Della Kincaid, who'd bought the store from Daddy years ago after leaving the newspaper business in Washington, D.C., still hadn't lost her reporterly ways of wheedling information outta people.

While at the library, I found a book by some doctor who treated people with what she called post-traumatic amnesia. No question in my mind that was what Alder had, what with the nasty wound on his head and his loss of memory. The doctor also talked about outbursts, something she said were to be expected. The book said to take things slow so the patient didn't feel pressured and blow up. Well, Alder was already doing that, something we later came to call his ups and downs.

That evening I showed Alder a list of questions in the book, and we spent the better part of an hour going over them. Nothing triggered anything more than irritation—or sorrow. Like when I asked if he was married. He just shrugged as he looked at his left hand. No sign of a ring. Then with pitiful hopefulness he added, "Whoever hit me on the head could've stolen the ring. Or maybe I didn't wear one. Many men don't." I looked at my left hand and thought I could still see a pale line round the third finger.

We carried on with the questions, and I asked if he was from Charlotte or Asheville or even Boone. Maybe he was a professor at the university there. Nothing. When I asked if he dreamed, he paused to think about that a while. "It's odd, isn't it? I know people dream, but I don't know if I do … or did. I know I need to eat and exercise to get well, but I don't know how I handled that in the past. It's as though I understand how to be a human being on some basic level, but nothing personal. I still have no idea who I am."

Chapter 5
Abit

MOLLIE TOOK TO ALDER like he was family. Of a morning, when I'd take his breakfast out, he'd open the door and she'd trill, something she saved for only a few special people. And she'd lay down next to him while he hung out in the woodshop. He wasn't quite ready to work yet, he said, but he wanted to study what I did so he'd could help when the time was right.

"Don't get in his way," I scolded Mollie more than a time or two. "Leave him be," I'd add to show I really meant it. It took me more than a coupla days to admit just how jealous I was of all the attention she was giving him. Hard to watch her carry on like that. But then a few nights later, when I was drifting off to sleep with Mollie's back warm against mine, I realized her doing that with Alder was exactly why I loved dogs so much.

Not long after that Alder came by my woodshop saying he was up for work. "I feel almost like my old self—if only I knew who that was. What can I do?"

Ever since Shiloh'd left I'd been meaning to run an ad for an assistant, but I'd feared what that might bring to my doorstep. I hated the idea of turning anyone down as much as I dreaded interviewing them in the first place. I showed Alder how to sand the right way (there's more to it than rubbing sandpaper all over something), and he sat down and started in. We worked together in a pleasant silence.

The quiet was shattered by a spate of dog barking. Mollie rarely barked, but I recognized her sound. Along with anothern's.

A hound almost twicet her size was half walking, half crawling cross the meadow that ran between the creek and the house. I pulled Mollie to the house and pushed her inside; she was offended, but I figured she'd just make matters worse. Then I called to Alder.

We headed down to the dog, now lying still, wet and filthy. I got some of Mollie's food and brought it over in her bowl. Poor old thing wolfed that down in no time. At first he ate lying down, his head nearabout lying in the bowl. But by the last licks he was standing. I carefully felt all round, and nothing seemed broken or wounded. He was just give out. We walked him over to Mollie's water bowl, and he lapped a little, but I reckoned he'd had plenty of water from the creek. There was no question in my mind that dog had followed Alder's trail here.

I patted the dog's head and checked his eyes and mouth. "I believe it's an Irish setter."

(Wouldn't you know an *Irish* dog would wander onto Fiona's old homeplace?)

"Looks that way," was all Alder said, but I could tell something was stirring inside him. In a while, we headed back to the woodshop. The dog curled up and slept the rest of the day outside the shop, too tired to go any farther.

Oncet a day had passed, and Mollie got over the insult of another dog using her bowls, she fell under his spell. She'd never had a canine friend, other than occasional visits from Della's Rascal. She watched as we gave it a bath. looking mighty pleased it wasn't her turn in the tub. (After the first couple hugs and pats, neither Alder nor me had wanted to get too close. Mud, burrs, and things we didn't want to identify were clinging to his fur.) Afterwards, while he was drying out in the sun, Mollie started kinda bothering him, and he snapped at her, just the way dogs do.

We left them to sort things out and went back to work. It was a hot day, so I'd kept the door to the shop wide open. I was deep into a dresser and needed something like six hands to keep everything in place. I didn't want to let go of the joint I was working on, so I called out to Alder, "Give me that chisel, would you?"

"Which one?"

Just then the board slipped and pinched my hand. "The RED one!" I shouted.

Before Alder could take offense, that sleepy old hound ran inside. One mystery solved.

"I reckon his name is Red," I said, stating the obvious.

Alder didn't have much to add, though I knew he was trying to figure out how he was related to the dog, which was about to lick the features offa his face. When he gently pushed it aside, he had tears in his eyes. "I don't know where he came from or why he was lost, but I know this is my dog."

We took that as a good sign, that things were starting to fire again inside his head. Leave it to a dog to open you up to see who you are. Or at least shepherd you in that direction.

"Does he have a chip?" I asked. Mollie had one, and I got excited this could solve the whole mystery of who Alder was. Of course, Alder didn't recall something like that, and the dog had long lost his tags. "I can take him to my vet," I offered. "Just say he wandered up, which he did. I can't take him today, but tomorrow for sure."

Early the next morning, Alder brushed Red and cut out more mats before we loaded him in the truck. Mollie looked worried as I drove off with Red taking her place on the passenger seat. I glanced in the rearview mirror and saw Alder consoling her as we disappeared down the drive.

It was late morning by the time I got back. Both Alder and Mollie hurried to the top of the drive. I stopped the truck and let Red jump out. He and Mollie started tussling and carrying on. Alder looked at me with such hope and anticipation, I struggled to find the right words. Finally I just blurted out, "No go. I'm sorry, but you never got that dog chipped." It came out like a scolding, and to be honest, I did feel irritated. Seemed funny to me a persnickety person like Alder had shown himself to be hadn't done that. Which dashed my hopes of finding out who *he* was. Or whether Red was even his dog.

Alder's disappointment dragged down his shoulders as he headed to his room. Red stopped playing with Mollie and ran after him. I watched as they went inside and the door closed. I wondered why Mollie hadn't joined them, though I was awfully glad she'd stayed by my side. I'd seen how different she'd become with Alder and Red round the farm. And I'd long known she woulda loved to live somewhere with children and other dogs close by. I felt a stab of guilt that she'd contented herself with my solitary life. Maybe I shoulda found her a better home where more was going on. I chewed on that for some time. After a while, I wondered who I was to think less of Alder for not getting Red chipped.

Chapter 6
Abit

OVER THE YEARS I'D gotten better at cooking. I learned how to make a mean Brunswick Stew, and Vern showed me how to bake biscuits and cornbread (though like I said, that still turned out pretty dry). And I tried new recipes I'd found at the library in ladies' magazines. I'd sneak them to a table (tucked inside *Popular Woodworking*) and copy recipes to bring home. Our favorites were garlicky greens with ham and a vinegary barbecue chicken I made on the stone grill out back.

But Alder's cooking turned out to be better than anything I'd tasted since I'd visited Alex Covington, Della's ex-husband/now boyfriend in D.C. (That was before he'd moved in with Della in Laurel Falls. Their story is kinda complicated.) Alder had healed up pretty good, at least on the outside, so most days he spent half his time in my shop and half in the kitchen. I was happy with the results from both places; I'd even put on a pound or two. Hard to tell if he was recalling recipes he used to make, or making up good ones on the spot, but they were all fine, filling the kitchen with rich smells. That day he'd pulled together a simple meal—grilled cheese sandwiches with homemade tomato basil soup from vegetables outta the garden.

And after a couple of rough starts, he'd gotten a gentle touch with the sandpaper. He seemed especially taken by my marquetry, something I'd let slide due to its fussiness and my lack of patience. Oncet he'd gotten more of his strength back, he started sketching a design that had potential. I made a few corrections and showed him where the veneers were. We figured he musta been an artist of some kind, given his sense of design. The way I figured it, now that he was surrounded by the majesty of the natural world, he felt called to capture those feelings in wood. Not unlike the way young'uns are drawn to catch fireflies in a jar, eager to hold that wonder close.

His enthusiasm gave me a bad feeling about the way I'd let my business run down—and everything else, to be honest. But I'd needed to get my strength back too. After our meal, over some perked coffee, Alder and I talked, and he helped me take a broader view of things. He was good at seeing the bigger picture, like the way he said that people weren't just buying my finished product but what I'd brought to it. I had to write down the way he put it to get it right. "They aren't buying just the aesthetics of the piece, but your intellectual and contextual prowess. People want to know a local artist used local wood in an original design." When he put it that way, I felt a little better.

That evening I picked up my mandolin, something else I'd let slide. It felt good to feel the notes beneath my fingers, and the music seemed to calm Alder. He even did a little toe-tapping.

Years ago, Fiona and I had started a bluegrass band—the Rollin' Ramblers—and I wanted to get back to playing with them. The band had canceled a few gigs when Fiona left and took her fiddle with her. But round here fiddlers were a dime a dozen. Nearabout every granny on down could make that instrument sing. The band found a good replacement in Ida Lee Jaffrey. She had a natural, relaxed way about her the rest of band members appreciated. Not as prickly as Fiona was about our sound. When I couldn't get it together to play my music, the band found what they called a *temporary* mandolin player who'd moved nearby from Kentucky. I reckoned I'd better get in some practice time if I didn't want them to make my replacement permanent.

Actually it wasn't *my* mando. It belonged to Fiona and her family, passed down for generations. She'd sent the boys home last time with a message that I'd better find anothern because she would soon be calling the loan back in. I ignored her. She'd have to come pry it outta my hands, and I knew she didn't want to get that close.

After playing a few lively favorites like "Liberty" and "Appalachian Mountain Girl," I set the mando back down. I had something else on my mind.

"Have you ever noticed how life goes back and forth between good and bad? Like when you break your ankle, which seems bad, but that means you don't have to take a job you didn't want in the first place."

Heat rose up his neck and colored his face; his tone matched it. "Are you saying my not knowing who I am is a good thing?"

"Well, I reckon that depends on who you were *before*."

He thought about that for a while. Then a slight smile creased his face. "This good/bad jockeying you're talking about, what could possibly be good about what's happened to me?"

"We'll have to wait and see, won't we? Maybe you needed a change in direction, but you weren't doing anything about it."

"And if I have a wife ..." He looked at his left hand again, as if it might've grown a ring since the last time we talked like this. "... she's missing me terribly."

"Maybe not."

"What? You think my wife tried to kill me?"

"Turn on the TV or pick up a newspaper. It happens all the time. We need to know more."

I could tell I'd messed with his head, but I had to get his attention. We needed help finding out who he was. "I haven't told a soul about you, but I want to bring Della Kincaid in on this. She used to be a crime reporter in D.C., and back in the day this would be right up her alley. Even all these years later I know she could help us find out who you are."

He wasn't having it. "I'm not ready for that," he said, all fidgety. "I need to discover who I am before I go public with even well-intended people, let alone the police. No telling what they might find."

"You sound like me, expecting something terrible," I said, drinking the last of my beer. "You know, it's just as likely you're heir to a fortune or owner of a big company."

"Not likely, Abit. This knot on my head says something untoward took place."

I wanted to tell him refined people fall into troublemaking as much as any others. I'd seen it firsthand. But then he rubbed his head and just like that had a fit of temper. "Ow! It still really hurts. Did you do this to me?"

Weird to watch him flash from calm to all agitated. I'd thought as time passed maybe he wouldn't keep having those ups and downs that book talked about, but here we were, smack in the middle of one. "Uh, well, I bet that does hurt," I said, trying to steer the conversation away from his outburst. "I can change the bandage for you."

"I'm not letting you anywhere near it," he said, his lip curling.

Oh man, what had I gotten myself into? I sat there kinda stunned. And worried.

After a while, when I reckoned the pain had eased, he said, "I'll start paying room and board soon. Somehow." He paused and added, "If not now, I will later, when I find out I'm heir to that fortune you were talking about."

He was trying to smooth things over, but I still felt uneasy when I went to bed that night. I tossed and turned. Part of me understood his angry outbursts. I'd feel out of sorts if I didn't even know my name. But what about when my boys came home and found a strange man in our home, losing it? If they got scared and called Fiona, she'd have them packed and moved to Asheville in no time.

Chapter 7
Della

"HOWDY, STRANGER," I CALLED out as Abit came through Coburn's front door. He looked around, nervously, as though he thought someone was following him. "I mean you, Abit. It's been a while."   -

"Oh, yeah. The larder's getting mighty low."

That threw me. He didn't sound like himself, as though he were reading from a script. I felt a shiver run through me, afraid I was losing touch with my boy. (That's what Alex and I called him, mostly in private, but he'd heard us say it a time or two.) I'd moved to Laurel Falls back when Abit was only 15 years old, and we'd saved each other's lives. And no, that wasn't an exaggeration. Over the years we'd spent a lot of time together, and in some ways, I knew I'd helped guide him toward a life that was fuller. Part mountain, part world-wise. Both suited him.

I came around the counter and gave him a big hug. Rascal, my little feist, scrabbled around his feet, begging Abit to pick him up. He must have left Mollie at home—another strange occurrence—but it gave Rascal a chance for more attention.

"Where've you been?" I asked as I made my way back to the cash register. Myrtle Ledford was ready to check out, though I knew she was just as eager to hear what Abit had been up to. He'd had a rough year, and we were both hoping things were smoothing out for him.

"Oh, trying to get back into the swing of work. Without Shiloh egging me on, I'd gotten kinda slack. But I balanced my checkbook the other evening and figured I'd better get on the stick."

"I know that feeling," Myrtle chimed in.

"You're looking better," I said. "Putting on some much-needed weight."

"Yeah, I'm feeling better. Doing more round the house. Conor and Vern will be back in a coupla weeks, so I want things in good shape by then."

We talked for a while, and it felt great to spend time with him. He'd even shut me out this past year, though I didn't take it personally. Just missed him. After Fiona left, I tried to help, but we had a spat about something I probably never should have said. We almost never exchanged harsh words, but that time Abit was so mad at me, I didn't hear from him for two weeks.

I'd told him that I could finally say it—I'd never liked Fiona. I thought it would make him feel better—reminding him she wasn't such a good catch after all. Or maybe that's just what

I told myself to ease my regret for shooting off my mouth.

"You think you're telling me something I didn't know?" he'd grumbled that day.

"What do you mean?"

"I could see through you as good as that plate glass window," he'd said, pointing to the front of the store. "Both Fiona and I knew you weren't crazy about her. Remember when I wrote that song for her, 'My Thorny Irish Rose'"?

"Yeah, when she left you for that doctor. I rest my case."

"No, I rest *my* case. You kept referring to that song as 'My *Horny* Irish Rose.' It was embarrassing."

"I'd forgotten about that," I mumbled, trying to sound contrite. But he knew me too well and could see me straining to hold back a smile. Wrong of me, I know, but I never could forgive her for the way she'd dumped him the first time for that prick in a Porsche.

I was brought back to present day by a delivery from Old Man Clendenin for some dilly beans his wife made for the store. He was a big guy, three hundred pounds at least, and for some reason everyone always stuck Old Man in front of his name.

"You doing okay over there?" I called out after Clendenin left. Abit had gone off to the spice aisle, seemingly lost in thought. I could see he had a long shopping list, but he wasn't making much progress. He just nodded. I got busy with other customers. When I looked up after a flurry at the register, I saw Abit standing there, ready to check out.

"You sure have a lot of groceries here, Abit. And some of them will spoil before the boys come home in a couple of weeks." He gave me a startled look. I didn't know what was going on with him, but he was obviously still working through some stuff. "You'd better watch out. You eat all of this, and you'll fill out those overalls like Old Man Clendenin."

I expected him to laugh. Most days, he liked my sense of humor. But this time he paused and went kind of pale. "Della, I need to tell you something."

"Hold on a minute, Honey. Here comes Elbert Totherow with ten cases of sourwood honey. Give him a hand, would you?" He quickly looked over that way. I figured he was more interested in seeing Elbert's daughter, Annie, who now pretty much managed Coburn's for me. Too bad it was her day off.

When they finished unloading, Elbert and I got busy settling what I owed him. Then he started telling me about his great-grandbaby's latest antics. I was laughing when I looked up and saw Abit wave on his way out the door.

Shoot! I missed my chance to ask him what he was making with capers and cumin.

Chapter 8
Abit

I'D WANTED TO TELL Della all about Alder so she could help us find out who he was, but when I'd finally gotten up the nerve, Elbert showed up and my courage deserted me. I'd tried to set up why I was buying so much stuff by telling her about the boys' return. Of course, nothing got past her, likely why she'd been such a good reporter. And I caught her looking funny at some of the ingredients Alder had put on the list.

Alder had just about emptied the freezer and pantry. Not that I was complaining. He'd made some awfully good meals: Beef Bourguignon (a dish he pronounced like a Frenchman), Pecan-crusted Trout, and something called Eggplant Moussaka. I couldn't believe such things could come from my garden and kitchen. Other than the trout from my neighbor, the ingredients were all at hand.

Mollie was getting more morsels too. I caught her begging—and Alder giving in, especially when cooking chicken, her favorite. But she didn't like every tidbit that made its way to the floor. We'd been eating more salads than usual, and any number of times I found clumps of chewed lettuce she'd probably pounced on, only to later spit out in disappointment. That always made me laugh.

Down the road a piece, I remembered I hadn't found any green peppercorns and rice vinegar. Alder had even underscored them. I hadn't seen them at Della's and didn't want to make too big a fuss about things I'd never use. She'd've definitely made a wisecrack. I headed to the SuperMart out on the highway, though I doubted they had them, either.

No question Alder was a city guy. I'd seen it before when people like that moved here or even just stayed a while. They got all upset when they couldn't find strange ingredients they were used to. As if the recipe couldn't limp along without them. And as if we didn't have things that made up for that in spades. Like the dappled sun dancing on the road ahead of me after making its way through a thick canopy of trees.

I'd planned to just run in and out of the SuperMart, but some guy was in there blocking the aisles. At first I couldn't figure what was going on, but it turned out he was shopping for his wife, and she made him show her all the brand choices on the shelves by taking pictures on his cellphone and sending them to her. It seemed every aisle I went down, there he was, standing in the way 'til his blamed email went through. At that moment I was glad to be single (though Fiona was never like that).

Finally on my way out—they didn't stock either of those things—I passed a display of quilted vests, the kind that have a bunch of pockets for whatever you need to carry with you. I knew it was really for fishermen, but I saw city folks wearing them so they didn't have to use a backpack (or worse, one of those man purses). Anyways, I bought one I thought would fit Alder and picked up some underwears for him too. He couldn't keep wearing my boy's. I also thought about getting him some razors. He'd grown a stubbly beard that he kept scratching at.

On the drive home, I started thinking about how people gave off clues about themselves if you stopped long enough to notice. I knew because I'd been a watcher my whole life. I pulled over to the side of the road and stopped the truck. I wanted to think more about that. We already knew Alder was well-educated and had soft, uncalloused hands. He definitely carried himself like someone who had not toiled, or at least not so he'd hurt his back. And those words that flowed outta his mouth so easy? Strange and exotic to me, though I liked hearing them. Lugubrious. Supercilious. Obfuscate.

Something about Alder made me picture him standing proud in a tweed jacket. Again, not like Nigel Steadman who wore custom-tailored suits, flashy in a way that would never suit Alder.

No, Alder had a solid, serious way about him that spoke of an accountant or even a lawyer. His mind was sure keen enough; he picked up on things faster than I ever could. Like birdwatching. When we'd see a bird I didn't recognize or remember, I'd be scrambling for the guidebook when he'd say rose-breasted grosbeak or blue-gray gnatcatcher. Like a teacher. Yeah, that was it. I'd asked him before about that, but it hadn't triggered any memories.

All those things were there for the viewing, which I supposed was why we had to keep him hidden for now. We just needed to figure out how and where they all came together. I hadn't shared any of these thoughts with him. They were just mine, and while I could help him on his journey back, he had to figure out who he was on his own. We all did.

When I finally made it home, Alder was all hepped up.

"I found something."

"What? Where?"

He was waving a newspaper in my face. "Here. In the *Citizen-Times*. A drug deal gone wrong. Don't ask me why, but this made the hair on my neck stand up."

"But this happened day before yesterday. You've been here almost a coupla weeks."

"No, no. What I mean is it *reminded* me of something. It must have; otherwise why did I get a buzz from it?"

I got a whole lot more than a buzz. I felt a jolt of fear run down my backside as I read about drug deals and shootouts in bad parts of town. Who had I brought into my home? Was drug dealing how he could afford those fancy clothes he'd showed up in? I'd met that kind of gangster before—like Clive Ownbey in England, who acted all polished and refined, but was a dangerous thief and killer.

I didn't want to dwell on this. I had groceries thawing in the truck, and for now, Alder was just Alder. We'd deal with it later. "We'd better get the food put up, and then we can talk."

I'd never seen someone so happy over groceries. He marveled over the capers and cardamon. He loved the dried figs and Japanese mushrooms. While he turned to place the curry powder into the pantry, I got the vest outta the bag. I wasn't sure if he was a drug dealer or not, but I'd bought the dang thing for him, so I figured I might as well give it to him. "Don't know if it's the right size. Hope so."

"You purchased this for me?" At first he seemed irritated. Probably one of his ups and downs or maybe he didn't like to feel beholding. But his moodiness slipped away oncet he tried it on. (It fit!) He stood in front of the mirror above the sideboard in the living room, and I could tell he thought he looked good.

"Thank you, Abit, I really mean it ... but no, it doesn't remind me of anything."

He'd read my mind. "Okay, but does it seem like something you would've worn before?"

"No, it doesn't. Not in the least."

And there we were again, like I'd offended him. Didn't matter. I was getting used to that—and it was still a clue of sorts. We already knew he was dressed fancy when he'd arrived, so more than likely that wasn't a fluke. On one level, I felt let down. On anothern, I knew we were getting somewhere.

Chapter 9
Abit

THAT EVENING ALDER MADE a fine dish he called Chicken Piccata. While he chopped some onions real fine, I noticed he started crying. I didn't think much of it. I mean, who doesn't when cutting up onions? But he looked bewildered.

"What's up?" I asked.

"Not sure. The onions aren't even stinging my eyes, yet I have tears."

"And you're sure you don't mind all this cooking?"

He gave a sad little chuckle. No mirth, closer to sorrow. "It feels like I've done this so many times before, only what's coming to me is not cooking for anyone else, just for me. Alone."

We were both quiet after that. I could see there was a sadness about him, something so deep his amnesia couldn't erase it. After a while, I set the table and opened a coupla microbrews I'd picked up at Coburn's. They weren't all bitter or grapefruity like some—just a nice nutty taste. When I tucked into the chicken, I didn't even need a knife. And when I chewed my first bite,

I couldn't believe how good those little green capers were. Everything about drug dealers was forgotten. For the time.

Afterwards, we sat outside watching the heat lightning. I'd always loved the way the clouds glinted and glowed, all pink and gray, edged with tinges of silver. Thoughts about him being a city boy were confirmed when Alder said he'd never seen anything like that. They'd been part of every summer my whole life (though that didn't stop me from marveling at them).

It was hard carrying on a conversation with someone who had no past. We'd already talked about our day, so there really wasn't much to say to one another. Our silence was pleasant enough, especially with the light show going on, but after a while, Alder said, "Tell me about your boys."

I could've talked forever on that subject. And I probably shared more than I should have, especially if he turned out to be some kinda drug dealer or con artist … and believe me, I knew about them. When I was at the Hicks (the Hickson School of American Studies, where I went to school in Boone), a trio of con artists led me on a dangerous chase through the hills of Virginia when I was trying to recapture my money and my reputation.

Anyways, I told him how fine Conor sounded on the fiddle—ever since he was a little tyke. Vern wasn't very musical, but we'd encouraged him in all the things he was good at, like sports and cooking. He loved to help both me and, back in the day, his mother in the kitchen. At first he made some disasters that still made me chuckle, but he'd kept at it.

I also told Alder about that kid I'd met in England a few summers ago. Baldy—short for Archibald, which I had to agree was no kind of name for a kid. That brought back long-ago memories of when I told Della that kids should form a panel for parents to run names by *before* they named their babies. Sure would save a lot of heartache in the schoolyard and hallways. Like a little girl we knew named Astrid, who got stuck with the nickname Ass Turd. And Richard Everhardt, for heaven's sake. Parents needed to think about things like that.

"Did you stay in touch with him?"

"Who?" I'd gone off thinking about the past, something Alder couldn't do. "Oh, Baldy. Sorta. I get a report about oncet a year. He's doing okay with a good foster family. He was one of the lucky ones."

I kept talking. Words just tumbled out, like I'd been saving them all for that moment. "I'm grateful the boys chose to stay here to finish their schooling where they grew up. And I'm happy for them that they get down to visit their mama in Asheville, so they can explore beyond the confines of our farm and town. They're well-versed in the natural life of birds and trees and wildflowers, so they'll never forget their roots."

I stood up. "Better yet, I'll show you some pictures." I headed inside to the sideboard where a picture of Fiona and the boys sat on top. I rarely looked at that photo; it was just for the boys, something to pretend there were no hard feelings. I reached into the cabinet and grabbed a shoebox full of snapshots.

We pored over them, me adding stories to go with each one. Alder made polite comments like, "I see Conor got your red hair" or "Vern doesn't look like you or his mother." That was when I explained how Fiona had red hair too and Vern was adopted. Why he was adopted wasn't something I wanted to get into, especially not knowing just who Alder was. But he was a good listener, and at some point, I had to stop myself. "I could talk about the boys 'til the cows come home."

"I thought you didn't keep animals." He took things awful literal sometimes.

"My point exactly. I could talk about them forever."

It took him a minute to get my joke. He chuckled. "Sounds like you're putting a brave face on things."

After his spell with the onions, I figured we both were. "Well, that's what you do, isn't it? You either keep on going or you don't. I've thought about not going on, more times than I care to admit. But then I wouldn't see the boys at all." And for some strange reason, that made me laugh. Not chuckle to appear happy, but a real laugh.

"Feels good to talk to someone else, doesn't it?" Alder said.

"You sound like a therapist. Do you think that's what you were? Are?"

"I doubt it. Don't feel it in my bones. Besides, when does stating the obvious require credentials? Do you have anyone to talk to usually?"

I nodded. "Yeah, Della Kincaid. You've got to meet her."

"We'll see."

Chapter 10
Abit

"YOU NEED A NAME."

Alder and I often went our separate ways after supper, but that evening I'd invited him to hang out round the fire in my living room. (It was a cool, rainy night, so a small fire felt right.) I didn't want him thinking he was a prisoner in a converted barn. We had the TV on, but since there was nothing worth watching, I'd turned the sound way down. That's when I mentioned about his needing a proper name.

"I've been thinking the same thing," Alder said, scooting his chair closer to the fire. "I can tell it's hard to keep calling me *hey* or *you*. And maybe a name will give me a sense of identity. Nomenclature is important to the human psyche."

"There you go again. Nomenclature," I offered, trying the word out on my tongue. "You're no wastrel; you've got some education behind you. Nobody talks like that otherwise." He chuckled, but his mirth died in his throat. He was still a stranger to himself. "I've been calling you Alder in my head," I confessed. "That's how

I found you, when I was down at the creek cutting them down. And you look like an alder.

"How's that?"

"Well, you're not overly tall and kinda delicate." I thought that hadn't come out right, so I added, "No offense."

"None taken."

I'd gotten us each a beer, though Alder didn't seem to care for his. I didn't much blame him given I was back to the cheap stuff 'til I could get to Coburn's again. I tipped the glass bottle his way. "Okay, I know one thing. You don't look like a Bud."

"No, I agree. Maybe Buddy?" he asked. We looked at each other and shook our heads.

"You need something more sophisticated."

"Okay, I've got an idea. Unmute the TV, and the next name we hear is mine."

"What if we come upon Oprah?"

He laughed. "Let's just see what happens. And, of course, I get first right of refusal."

I grabbed the remote and soon we heard the announcer say the eleven o'clock news was fixing to start. I looked at my watch, surprised how fast time had slipped by.

"Good evening, this is Matthew Hudson with your eleven o'clock news."

"Matthew," Alder mimicked, trying it on for size. He thought a while before adding, "Not Matt. Matthew."

I liked that name. Suited him, and Matthew was my favorite book in the Bible. I was

comfortable calling him that, and it appeared
Matthew was too. He was smiling again, and I
could see his lips moving, saying the name over
and over. I reckoned that was as good a way to
name yourself as any.

"Just use the Matthew part," I added. "Don't
take on Hudson."

And wouldn't you know it? That set him off.
He stood up, all full of himself, like he was
gonna challenge me to a dual. "I don't plan to
steal anyone's identity, Bradshaw." Then he sat
down again and went back to watching the news,
like nothing strange had just happened.

"You don't really need a surname. Not round
here," I said, trying to lighten things up. "You
can hold out 'til you remember your real one."

We sat quiet-like for a while, until I started
yawning my head off. I looked over at my new
neighbor, Matthew, dressed in high-water pants
and a flannel shirt, his salt and pepper hair
growing long and shaggy round the collar and
his beard still kinda straggly. I shook my head
at the strangeness of it all.

Of course, who was I to talk? With no one
round to care, I'd kinda let myself go too.

Chapter 11
Abit

THE NEXT DAY FELT like the one before it, and the one before that. Looking back, I should've appreciated the calm, given the storm that was about to wash over us. But at the time, I longed for something to happen. Matthew hadn't remembered anything more about his past, and we both felt kinda stuck out here on the farm.

That morning we'd worked together as usual, then he'd left the woodshop and, I'd assumed, gone to his room. We'd agreed to get our own lunch; all the fuss and mess from even his grand cooking could feel like a burden from time to time.

When I finished up for the day, I looked round for him. He wasn't in his room. Or the house, when I went in to change out of my dusty clothes. *Maybe he went for a walk*, I thought. By the time I came downstairs, though, I caught a whiff of something fine on the stove. "Smells good," I said as I came into the kitchen.

"The least I could do." Matthew stopped stirring and turned off the gas. "Listen, Abit, I was way out of line last night. I don't know what comes over me. Later, as I contemplated my impropriety and all that's transpired this week, I got a strong feeling that I need to go back."

I had to admit that part of me was ready for him to leave. "Okay, but you don't know where to go back to."

"No, what I mean is, I want *us*, if you'll help me, to retrace my steps. Try to find out how I got here. I think that's the best way to get rid of me too."

I waved off that last comment. (Was I that obvious?) As I thought about the other, I finally said, "You're talking about a needle in a haystack. Over yonder, where I figured you'd come from, is the Laurel Falls Wilderness, thousands of acres of serious forest."

He turned on the gas again and went back to stirring. "We could walk the creek and see if anything comes to me."

I wasn't too keen on the idea, but I nodded just to move on. I needed to think about how we could cover enough ground in that vast wilderness to do any good. I left to feed the dogs their supper.

When I came back, again I couldn't find Matthew. I called out his name, but no answer. It wasn't 'til I looked out the kitchen window that I saw him outside, fussing with our barbecue grill.

"Whatcha cooking there?" I said as the screen door slammed behind me.

"Come see for yourself. And get your arm ready."

He'd rummaged through the pantry and come up with pinto beans that were bubbling in a dutch oven nestled in the coals (when did he start this fire?) and a table nearby with our cutlery, plates, and some corn relish I remembered a neighbor giving me last Christmas. I couldn't recall why I hadn't long ago doused my beans with it. He'd also made coleslaw and had hot dogs threaded onto sticks he'd whittled to a point.

On a stump off to the side, our ice cream churn sat next to two chairs. I couldn't remember the last time we'd used it. The old wooden slats still looked good, but the rust on the crank worried me. Matthew set me up with a beer and disappeared into the barn with the churn. When he returned, he'd done a makeover good enough for one of those makeover TV shows. Luckily, we had everything we needed—I kept rock salt for all kinds of reasons round the farm and blocks of ice in the freezer in case the power went out. Matthew had chipped away at the block with an ice pick.

He'd made a bowlful of what Mama used to call boiled custard—that's what I'd smelled in the kitchen, rich with vanilla—and had it cooling in a bigger bowl of ice. All kinds of thoughts came to me, like why me and the boys hadn't used that churn in so long and how much

I'd love a big bowl of homemade ice cream right then. I laughed for the first time that day.

When I ate those hot dogs, I couldn't believe how good they tasted cooked over the fire, the smell of woodsmoke adding to the pleasure. I hadn't eaten hot dogs in quite some time; even the boys didn't ask for them, probably because we just boiled them, turning the water a sick reddish color. I pinched off two bits and gave them to Mollie and Red, who'd been begging and getting in the way.

After supper, we sipped more beer while I cranked. As I turned the handle, Matthew watched me careful-like. Seemed he'd never cranked ice cream before and didn't know exactly how to do it. In time, we put more ice and salt round the container and traded seats. We talked about things outta the past. Well, *my* past. I told him about some of the adventures Della and I had gotten into, and I could tell he was having trouble believing me. I would have too if I hadn't lived them.

Then, just like that, Matthew stopped cranking.

"Hey, no fair. You've gotta keep it up," I said. "We're not far off now."

He still didn't say anything, just sat there looking stunned. When I thought he was having anothern of his ups and downs, he said, "As I was cranking, I saw a whole scene, like a theater production in my head. The setting is not unlike now: hot, likely Southern. I'm at a church—I can see the sign in the front; it's an Episcopal church—and I'm with an older woman, who's dressed to the nines. Rings, diamond brooch, silk dress. She's standing before a red door."

"So you're slumming it here with me."

He kinda chuckled. "Could be. Who knows? Then again, maybe I blew all her money and I'm homeless."

"Not with pampered hands like that. But I'd call this a breakthrough—though you still owe me a bunch of cranks."

The sun was setting by the time we opened up that churn. In honor of the flavor we chose, the sky had turned the color of peaches: yellow, pink, and, well, peach. We saluted the sky and dove into that frosty container. The peaches and vanilla turned cream and eggs into heaven. So much so we both got an ice-cream headache.

"Ow," I said, rubbing my forehead. "I hope this doesn't freeze your brain any more than it already is."

"Oh, just the opposite, Abit. All kinds of things are coming to mind. I believe that woman was my grandmother. I wonder about the church and where that might be. I was just a kid, but still, it's a start."

After my headache eased, I went back to eating, though I slowed down a bit. We polished off more ice cream than we should have, but we kept saying it's not as good the next day. Even Matthew seemed to recall that.

I didn't know when I'd had this much fun. Sadness grabbed hold of me as I thought about how much Conor and Vern woulda loved this kinda evening. There would be plenty of warm weather left when they got back, and I made a vow to do more things with them before they were back in school.

I was startled when Matthew said, "I don't know when I've had this much fun. We could do this again when your boys come home." I kinda chuckled, but really, I was worried we were starting to read each other's minds.

I musta made a face because he said. "Are you ashamed for them to meet me?"

"Why would I be ashamed. It's just ..."

"What?"

"So much to explain."

"Do you have to?"

I thought for a minute. "Yeah, I do. I can't start covering things up with them. That's a slippery slope. But they'll get it. And they'll love Red, just wait and see."

Chapter 12
Abit

OF A MORNING, MATTHEW and I kept going through the newspapers, though nothing much ever came to light, at least as far as his predicament.

"I think I'd better cut back on the papers, cancel the *Watauga Democrat,*" I told him as I sipped a second cup of coffee. "It's time to go back to just the *Citizen-Times.* And with two mouths to feed now, plus two dogs, I'm thinking about letting that one go too.

"No, please. I'll pay you back ... when I can. We need to keep on top of things."

"We are on top of things, but there's nothing happening. Besides, it's been almost three weeks. You're old news by now."

"A little longer, please." He paused and added, "Or do you have a computer I could use?"

"Just an old one I use for my invoices and such. I'd love to keep up the subscriptions, but I'm not made of money, you know."

"Yes, but I am."

I laughed, but when I glanced over at Matthew, he looked like the dog who'd stolen the Sunday roast—both happy and scared. He seemed dumbfounded by what he'd just said.

I left him to think on it, not putting much faith in that idea, and headed out to the shop. After a while, Matthew joined me; we worked together the rest of the morning. He'd turned into a good helper. At first he didn't have much attention span, like his mind was off daydreaming, but lately, he'd gotten in a comfortable groove. Until.

I said something wrong, I can't even recall what, and he threw the piece of wood he was sanding across the room and let out a string of curses. Fortunately for him, the wood wasn't aimed at me, or I believe that would've been the end of our arrangement. I couldn't hold with that. I could excuse the ups and downs that doctor's book talked about, but not violence.

We stayed clear of one another the rest of the day, though he wasn't far from my thoughts. I just kept wondering if Matthew could be dangerous after all—and what I'd be exposing my boys to oncet they came home. I made my own supper, and I reckoned Matthew starved himself or ate the snacks I'd left in there that first day he'd arrived.

The next morning, Matthew skipped breakfast too. I left him to work through whatever was bothering him and picked up the *Citizen-Times* from the mailbox. When I finished the breakfast dishes, I sat down and opened to a front page that screamed in big bold type: Body Found in Wilderness.

I ran out to the barn, Mollie following close on my heels. "Matthew. Matthew. You've gotta open up."

When he wouldn't answer I got worried. I tried the door. Unlocked. "Matthew, you all right?" I called out, but as I eased the door open, I could see I was talking to an empty room. I noticed the grip I'd given him along with his clothes were gone. Mollie snuffled round like a bloodhound. Of course Red was gone too. I sat on his bed for a while, thinking about what this might mean, before heading back to the house.

I poured myself some coffee and reread the story. They hadn't identified the man yet, but he'd been dumped in the wilderness not that far from a trailhead parking lot. He'd been shot, and best they could tell he'd died somewhere else and then was moved to his final resting place. When I finished reading, I felt both burdened by the fact a killing had come so close to home, and relieved that Matthew had apparently left for a life as a drifter. I had to admit it would be nice not having all this trouble raining down on my life anymore. I let out a big sigh.

I worked all morning, and maybe because of my lighter heart, things went well. My dovetail joints came together the way I'd planned, the carving on the sideboard was some of my best, the lathe and I worked as one. I was back.

I couldn't figure why I'd abandoned my work when Fiona'd left. Especially after a day like this when I was reminded how many good feelings—happy, worthy, even clever—I got from turning out tables and hutches and beds. Maybe I'd held back because I feared the dark feelings trying to swallow me whole would taint whatever I made. But I didn't believe that. Things that came from my hands, *through* my hands were from somewhere good inside. I reckoned the fire in me had just gone out for a time.

As I headed to the kitchen to pull together some dinner, the air was pungent with the smell of rain. Pretty soon a drizzle turned into showers. I called Mollie, but she didn't come. Even calling out "Diiin-ner" didn't bring her running. Then I heard barking, and this time I knew it was hers. I grabbed my raincoat and followed the sound down the slope of my land as it eased toward the creek. I couldn't see anyone, but finally I noticed two dogs tussling the way they do. Mollie and Red. I walked a little farther and came upon Matthew sitting on the ground, his back against a couple of, what else, alders. The grip sat nearby.

"I didn't get very far," he said.

"Where in the world were you going?"

"Good question."

"Why?"

He stayed quiet for the longest time. I was about to ask again when he said, "After my outburst yesterday, dark thoughts took over. Then I remembered something." He paused and I had to ask what. He waved me away. "Not yet. Can't go there." He sat for a while and added, "I just wanted to get out of here. Move somewhere no one knew me. Where I couldn't bring harm."

I was about to ask him again what he'd remembered, but then something more pressing came to mind. "Haven't we come through enough by now for you to trust me?" I asked. "If we don't have that, I can't do much more of this."

"Exactly. That was why I was leaving." He held up the grip. "But this isn't enough to get me very far, as you said early on. And I'm too much of a wimp to try."

A heavy silence hung between us. I was feeling damp and achy from hunkering down, trying not to sit on the wet earth. I got up, knees creaking, and that's when I remembered the newspaper story. I told him about the body.

He shivered. "That's not far off from what I remembered," he said. "A body. And I fear I had something to do with it. Until now, I could convince myself I was an innocent in all of this."

It seemed I was always struggling with two minds. One was glad I'd found him, the other wished he'd gone and taken all this sorrow with him. I kept asking myself what if he were a vicious killer. And yet, somehow, I didn't believe it. Either way, it was time to get to the bottom of this. "We need to go to the wilderness," I told him. "Like you said the other evening."

Only now he was the one saying no. "Can't do that. The police will be everywhere."

"We'll be careful, dress you like a local," I said. His beard had filled out enough to give him a different look, and his clothes were already well-worn. "Besides, we'll be starting from here. They might be long gone by the time we make our way that far into the wilderness."

"But we're just two men against the system. We don't have any power, and I don't have any way of defending myself. I don't know what I did—or didn't do—and that could trap me in their net."

I shook my head. "Think about it this way—like the birds you've been watching. Haven't you seen how small birds can scare off raptors three or four times their size? It's amazing. We can do the same, if we're smart about it." Matthew didn't say anything, which I took as a good sign. I held out my hand to help him up. "Come on, let's go to the house and get you some dinner. And dry clothes. Again."

We neither one spoke a word on the way up, but as we got to the top, Matthew grabbed my arm. "Someone's coming."

Chapter 13
Della

WHEN I DROVE UP, Abit was standing near his barn, talking with a man I'd never seen before. Soaking wet. At least Abit had had enough sense to wear some raingear. The other man was dressed in flannel and denim that soaked up water like a sponge. And a fisherman's vest. A duffle bag at his feet. He looked like a local, but there was something odd about him. The clothes didn't fit quite right, and he seemed uncomfortable in them. Not unlike when Abit dressed our friend Nigel Steadman, a man known for sartorial splendor, from the dry goods store in Laurel Falls when he'd arrived without any baggage (at least of the physical kind). Nigel went on to get us both embroiled in his latest scheme. I could only hope this man wasn't of that ilk, but after the morning headline, my fears were he might be even worse.

When I'd read the whole article, a bad feeling had come over me. I thought about all that food Abit had bought, and my imagination went wild, picturing a band of men holding him hostage and eating him out of house and home. My fears soared with news of a body in the wilderness, which as the crow flies isn't that far from his farm.

I felt a little better when I actually saw Abit, but still, who was that guy? A drifter? Abit was too kind to those fellows. They weren't all out of a Woody Guthrie song.

As I turned off the engine, Abit walked over, positioning himself in a way that obscured my view of the man. I craned my neck and could see him edging toward the guestroom.

"Della, what brings you over here?" he asked. He sounded stiff as a spaghetti-western movie star.

I got out of my old Jeep Cherokee and held out the newspaper. Fortunately by then the rains had stopped. "Honey, I was worried about you. I read about the body, and come on, you and I both know you've been buying groceries for more than just you." I started to get a little choked up, and Abit put his arm around me. I dug my nails into my palms to stop the tears and pulled myself together. "I was worried you'd been too nice to some drifters who were up to no good." I crinkled the front page again for emphasis.

We headed to the porch, where we'd sat so many times before. Over the years, we'd shared good news and bad swaying on that swing. This time he told me all about the man who didn't know who he was. At first I thought it was just a ruse, and I told Abit he was putting himself in danger. "You don't know anything about this guy."

"No, *you* don't know anything about him," Abit said. "And he doesn't know much, either. But I *do* know something about him. He's been here a few weeks, and I don't believe he means me any harm." I think I tutted, involuntarily, and that was when he got red in the face and added, "Don't come out here telling me what I know or don't know."

Just then Mollie came running onto the porch to greet me—and looking for Rascal. I'd left him at home to cut down on the chaos, but now I was sorry I had. Next thing I knew a big Irish Setter was halfway in my lap. It broke the ice for us, and Abit and I both laughed. A little.

Abit was right. He hadn't been harmed over the weeks the drifter had been there, so it seemed unlikely the man was a threat. At least while he didn't know who he was—or why the police might be after him. Amnesia brought with it an innocence that could mean Abit was safe. For now.

I knew Abit was about to apologize for raising his voice. He often did that, even when he was in the right. I stopped him. I liked seeing him fight for his stance. "Honey, you're right. I overstepped. I was just so worried about you being out here all alone with a stranger."

"You knew all along, didn't you?"

"Well, I knew something was up. I couldn't quite see you making Trout Piccata for yourself."

"It was chicken."

I chuckled. I was so relieved I would have laughed at anything. "Okay, but when I read about the murder in the woods, I let my imagination run away."

Abit stood and walked toward the guestroom; he motioned for me to follow. The dogs came along without any encouragement. When he knocked on the door, there was no answer.

"Come on, Matthew, it's time you and Della met."

I could hear shuffling inside, and finally a middle-aged man came to the door. He adjusted his vest in a way that reminded me of Nigel, a practiced motion that seemed to come naturally. He nodded at me, and I nodded back. But then I opened my big mouth.

"Are you connected with this?" I asked, holding up the newspaper.

"I don't know. I hope not."

"We were just talking about heading into the wilderness to find out," Abit said.

"Oh," I said. And then before I'd thought it through, added, "I want to go with you." We hadn't had an adventure together in a long time, and I was eager to get at it again.

"No way, ma'am. I'm not going with a stranger."

That was Matthew, calling *me* a stranger. And *ma'am*. I could feel my temper rearing its head when Abit spoke to me as though I were Vern or Conor.

"Della, we need your help with some research. Back at Coburn's. Maybe Alex can join in too. I've got some notes at the house, and it would do us a world of good to make something more of these bits and pieces, maybe tie them together. But we need to retrace Matthew's steps on our own."

I hated that he was making perfect sense. I'd just be a third wheel on their trip through the wilderness. But I had to share one idea before I left. "You know you could use dental records to find out who you are. I can tell your choppers are in first class condition—whitened even—so someone has your records. Probably in Asheville or Charlotte."

"Of course I've considered that," Matthew said, more dismissively than I felt warranted. "I could have gone to the authorities right away if that were the direction I'd chosen. But I need to know first I'm not in danger." He hung his head and added, "Or whether I've done something despicable."

I had to admit his manner didn't seem like an act. I sat in my Jeep and pouted while Abit gathered the papers with the so-called leads on them. By the time he came back out, I'd cooled off and accepted the way things had played out.

And when I glanced at the list Abit handed me, I felt my pulse quicken.

I drove home almost as fast I'd raced to Abit's. I wanted to catch Alex before he got involved in some other project. We'd been colleagues in the newspaper world, back when it was booming. I'm glad I lived and worked during an era when journalism was respected and supported. Just saying the words "Fourth Estate" still gave me goosebumps. I knew down to my core how vital it is for framing facts and focusing light onto the darkness of man's machinations. Alex was the best investigative reporter I knew, which is why he'd won a Pulitzer. Okay, it was years ago, but he was still on his game.

Alex was staring at the computer screen when I got home. I'd called him from Hanging Dog to read him the list of leads Abit had given me.

"Any luck?" I asked.

"I'm good, but not that good. It's only been fifteen minutes."

I hadn't dealt with something this rich since that whistleblower put me onto the cartel that had snared Nigel into its web. But that was what? Five years ago? I was eager to dive into a new caper.

Alex and I made a good team, both personally and professionally. He'd been the managing editor of a magazine in Chapel Hill for a number of years, working fifty or sixty hours a week. A few months ago he cut back to only thirty. Since he mostly worked from home, he could easily maintain his magazine duties and still have time to work with me on this story.

"I want to check into the Episcopal church. I know that search will cough up a lengthy list, but it's a good place to start," Alex said as he stood and stretched. I looked at my watch and knew exactly where he was headed. The Rancillio espresso machine. Creature of habit. "I'll begin with Asheville and Charlotte. Of course he could be a tourist."

"No, I think you're on the right track. And is Google Street View good enough to show red doors?"

"Only one way to find out."

Chapter 14
Abit

MATTHEW AND I SLOWLY made our way down to the creek. We'd gotten up early to beat the heat, which meant we were both sleepy and pokey. But really it was more that neither one of us was in a hurry to revisit that place we'd first met. The wet weather over the past week had washed away any signs that a wheelbarrow had dug deep trenches into the soft ground as it carried Matthew to safety. I also felt put out those dang alders were already trying to take back the creek bank.

The dogs thought our walk was a grand excursion, but Matthew and I trudged along, both burdened by worry. After a while, though, I started to relax, telling myself we were just on a family hike. Family. Seemed I hadn't used that word in ages. I paused for a moment at the spot where I'd found Matthew lying in a heap. He didn't recall it, of course, but he somehow knew. We both stood silent, like funeral goers paying their respects. We didn't know it then, but in a way, someone had died there.

I looked over at Matthew, decked out in a floppy hat, one of my t-shirts, and the trousers that had been ruined by the creek—stiff and scratchy but at least not high-water pants—and wondered about the man who'd preceded Matthew. I couldn't even imagine what he might've looked like going to the office or school or whatever he did in that life.

As we walked, we came upon a place where the creek grew wider and the foliage held back. We stopped to admire the way the sun hit the water. Matthew said it brought to mind "hundreds of silver butterflies resting, awaiting their ascent." Spoken like an artist.

We were quiet after that, following the creek as it meandered right and left, up and down. Summer was at its fullest now, which in North Carolina meant suffocating overgrowth of everything green and natural. Matthew pulled out one of his big words—fecundity—which when he explained it to me fit the bill. This land with its rich soil plus plentiful sunshine and water couldn't stop growing. The soft smells of spring had turned raw and overripe.

"You're so good with words," I said as we made our way, "here's something that's confused me since I was a kid. If someone is ruthless, why isn't a nice person ruth? You never hear anyone called ruth. Things like that bother me."

He smiled, the way a teacher does at a thick student. "You've got a point there, Abit. But I'm sure you've heard its stem word rue, as in rue the day you did something. It means regret, of course. Ruthless is someone without regret. I have to admit, it does seem like a linguistic artifact."

I nodded my thanks. As we walked, we turned our attention to the birds fluttering in the trees above us. Carolina chickadees' noisy bursts of song. Pileated woodpecker's trumpeted call. But the red-tailed hawk's sharp cry reminded us we weren't on a leisurely walk. We moved on.

The trees grew denser and the path darker, which drew our eyes downward to steady our footfall. That was when Matthew spotted something light blue in the undergrowth. We'd brought some plastic bags from home, doing like we'd seen on TV. I didn't know if we were just playing at detective, but it seemed a good idea to protect anything we found. Holding a blue hanky with a bag over his hand, Matthew stared at it for a long time.

"Mean anything?" I asked. He shook his head. "Well, it looks like that fine fabric your dress shirt was made of. At least the same quality. I can't imagine many folks come hiking here with a hanky like that. Bandanas are more like it."

"Maybe so." He poked the hanky into the bag and sealed it. Neither of us had mentioned the blood on it. "Don't know it's mine. Don't know it's not," was all Matthew said before stuffing the bag into his backpack.

We'd gone pretty far, and I could tell Matthew was dragging. I told him to rest while I scouted the area round us. I saw all kinds of natural things worth noting—a stand of Jack-in-the-pulpits; tiny proud British soldier lichen covering a log; a few deep yellow mushrooms—but other than three cigarette butts that looked too old to matter and a coupla bottle caps, nothing seemed even remotely related to our investigation.

I headed back to Matthew, and we walked for another hour until we came to an opening. Usually in the wilderness, mostly you just saw trees. Not that that wasn't reward enough, what with their thick and varied foliage, but this spot had a vista of sorts, looking out toward range after range of mountains. I was happy to sit again and take it in.

"The atmospheric perspective is astonishing here," Matthew said. I wasn't exactly sure what that meant, but it backed up my ideas that he'd led a gentler sort of life filled with art and literature.

It was a good place to stop for a bite—just odds and ends from the fridge and larder. That's what Fiona always called the cupboards where we kept our canned goods, and I'd picked up some of her phrases over the years. Hard not to when you lived so close together. I reckoned, though, it was time I pared down my use of them. They sounded stupid to my ear now. Another piece of my life, as I knew it, gone.

I stood to signal it was time to get a move on. I gathered our paper bags and gave the scraps to the dogs, who were having so much fun they lifted my spirits.

"Are we within the boundaries of the wilderness?" Matthew asked. Like I was a walking GPS.

"Don't know for sure, but I believe we are. Smells like we are." Matthew looked at me funny. "Something about the wilderness has a different smell—from all the oxygen and less sunlight," I explained. I checked my map. "According to this, there's a parking lot up ahead, though I don't hear any people carrying on. I doubt we're near that crime scene where they found the body. That would be too easy. Still, we need to watch out. I'm sure the cops have a sizeable area marked off."

"Let's keep going," Matthew said, drinking the last of his water. He wasn't used to this kind of walking and didn't know to pace himself. I'd need to share my canteen on the way back.

"Okay, but remember, we've got to cover this same ground to get home. You up for that?"

He paused. "Well, maybe a little longer."

Along the trail, we heard a few crows making a racket, but that was about it. I often wondered where all the birds went when, at certain times, not a one was in sight. Resting, I reckoned. I jumped a little when Matthew broke the silence. "I know I keep asking this, but why do you believe me?" he asked.

I stopped walking and Mollie bumped into me. "Who says I do?"

"Oh, come on, Abit. Why would you be doing all this otherwise?"

I sighed. "I was just trying to lighten things up a bit. I guess because you don't seem like a killer. And the fact that body in the newspaper was found near a parking lot makes me think you were dumped at *this* parking lot—the other guy at a different one. The cops weren't looking for you, so they didn't come this way. That's why they didn't find the hanky."

"Maybe this isn't where I was dumped," he said. "Or maybe I don't have anything to do with that other body."

"Well, there is that," I said, sighing. It all felt so useless, as though we were going round in circles.

I was carrying both packs by the time we got close to home, Matthew dragging himself along, but, all in all, doing pretty good. I kept seeing those healthy backs of the dogs, wishing I could strap these packs to them. But that wasn't the rules dogs played by, at least not in our lives together.

When the farm was within our sights, Matthew stopped to catch his breath. After a time he said, "Something bad happened back there, but I don't know what. Strange as it sounds, I'm getting used to not knowing my own name. That I can deal with. What really worries me is the sense that no one misses me." I had no words to comfort him, but I soon realized he wasn't looking for that. He nodded his head and said, "I'll be okay," and I think he meant it.

In the end, we'd found only a hanky, but I'd found that I trusted this strange man more now than when we'd headed out. And I felt reacquainted with the natural beauty that surrounded my farm and that inspired my work. I had to believe that was progress.

Chapter 15
Abit

"OH NO! IT'S THE FBI!"

The color drained from Matthew's face when I called that out. "The FBI? You said no one came here," he growled. "But it's like Grand Central Station."

I couldn't argue with that. My only wish was all these folks had come by when I'd felt so alone.

Curtis Maynard parked in the drive near the guestroom, where he'd stayed a few year ago when I worked with the FBI to find that serial killer. I was pleased to see him, though nervous about pulling off Matthew's introduction. Fortunately, we started with the obvious.

"Where are those fine boys of yours? And where'd you get that good looking red dog?"

It'd been a while since I'd seen Curtis, but he knew about Fiona, so I didn't have to drag all that up again. I brought him up to date on the boys and told him Red belonged to my new assistant, Matthew. I motioned Matthew over. (He'd tried to get away and hide in the guestroom, but he hadn't been quick enough.)

"Matthew, I'd like you to meet my good friend, Curtis Maynard. He and I worked together a while back—and became friends."

Curtis stuck out his hand. They shook. "Does Matthew have a last name?" he asked, cracking a smile, though that didn't stop me from panicking. Matthew didn't miss a beat. "Ruisseau. Matthew Ruisseau." *Where in the world did he come up with that?* I wondered.

I felt stupid that I hadn't thought about Curtis coming this way oncet that body in the wilderness was found. That was part of the Pisgah National Forest, and of course the Charlotte Field Office where Curtis worked would take the lead.

We shot the breeze for a while, and when my nerves calmed down, I invited them to the house for some refreshment. It was late enough in the day for a beer to be in order. I didn't think Curtis noticed my jitters, but I sure saw the sweat on Matthew's brow. I wasn't surprised when he excused himself to finish up some work in the barn.

He'd barely closed the door when Curtis started in, asking me how I'd met Matthew and what I knew about his background.

"I know what I'm doing," I told him. "Try leaving your badge in the car from now on."

"Come on, Abit. You're a terrible liar. That guy is trying to look like a hillbilly in his t-shirt and jeans, but there's something about him that doesn't match. There's a refinement he's trying to hide."

"Well, that's better than being a low life and trying to hide that." I said. "You've been watching too much CSI. You think you're a profiler now."

"I *am* a profiler now. Just got back from Quantico. That's why I haven't been by lately."

We'd kept in touch over the past few year. Mostly when Curtis wanted to get outta Charlotte, which was often enough. He started in again, asking if I was up to my "junior detective work" again. Ha! Last time me and my buddy Wallis Harding solved the case for the FBI, so there was nothing *junior* about that. But I didn't want to get into it with him.

Things fell silent for a while, until Curtis said, "Abit, I was going to ask if I could use your guestroom. Just for a couple of nights. I'm too tired to drive home."

"I've rented it out to Matthew. Ever since Fiona left, I've been bad about not working enough. I needed the money."

He looked over thataway, kinda scowling at my choice of tenants. I was too nervous to think of the obvious, but Curtis was never shy. "Well, can I stay in the boys' room?"

"Yeah, sure. I think the sheets are even clean. I've been getting ready for their return."

"Can I go lie down now?" When I nodded, he added, "Thanks, Abit. I'm sorry I'm so irritable. I'll be better after a nap. Then I have to go back to work. I won't be in until late. Do you still have that extra key?"

"Oh, I'll just leave the door unlocked."

"Don't do that. No telling who's roaming these woods."

"I'll likely be up anyway. Don't sleep too good these days."

Chapter 16
Abit

"HOW IN THE WORLD did you come up with Ruisseau?" I asked.

Matthew was lying on his bed, hands behind his head with Mollie on one side and Red on the other. That looked a lot more comfortable than what I'd been doing. I'd breathed a sigh of relief when Curtis went back to work.

"It means creek in French," he said, sounding matter of fact.

"That doesn't answer my question. How did you come up with that on the spot?"

"I don't know. It just popped into my head."

"You sure seem to know French real good. You drop names like Beef Bourguignon and Salad Niçoise as easy as I say pinto beans and cornbread."

"I've noticed that myself. Somehow I knew it meant creek, which is where this chapter of my life began."

"Do you think maybe you were a French teacher somewhere? Or a translator?"

"It's something to look into. I speak French, I have a prodigious vocabulary, if I do say so

myself, and may have prospects of a wealthy
Episcopalian grandmother. I can see her now,
her soft hand in mine. And that big house with
the red door with brass numerals 1247 ...

"Wait a minute. You never said anything about
the door having a number."

"Oh. Maybe that came to me later." That
seemed to depress him.

I knew it had to be hard to start getting
breakthroughs, then realize so much was still a
mystery. But there was something he could be
grateful for: At least his granny's hands didn't
have prison tats or grease under her fingernails.

Our moment of peace didn't last long.

Next thing we heard the postman grinding
gears as he topped the drive. Matthew
nearabout pushed me out the door of my own
guestroom so I could deal with him.

I was relieved to see it wasn't Frankie Ivester
this time. Just some substitute I'd never met
before who didn't know who I was or who was
living here. All he cared about was getting rid of
a huge box addressed to me. I couldn't imagine
who'd sent me such a big package, but to be
honest, it was hard not to get my hopes up.

The box was too heavy to carry anywhere, so
I opened it right there in the driveway, using
my pocketknife to slice it open. I pulled back
the flaps and stared at a pile of junk. Odd pieces
of wood, scraps of fabrics I'd saved for cleaning
cloths, old blue jeans for the same purpose,
woodworking magazines. Stuff I'd kept more

outta laziness than usefulness. I dug round a little more, and all I got was a splinter. And a note:

No idea how I came to have this. Must be yours.

It wasn't signed, but it didn't need to be. Fiona.

I piled it all back in the box, threw it in the truck bed, and headed straight for the dump. It was late in the day, so I prayed it was still open. I didn't want to hold on to that crap one minute longer than I had to. I let out a sigh when I saw the gates open, pulled through, and parked near the edge. I heaved it over, and the heavy box exploded as it landed in the sad, sorry pit. The only satisfaction I got was the postage stamp said it cost her eighteen dollars to send me that crap. And I took some comfort that her note didn't mention anything about returning her mandolin.

It was kinda funny. We hadn't officially divorced yet, and I knew the day was coming that I'd need to pay her for half of the farm, but I dreaded returning that mando more than turning over all that money.

WITH A RARE FEELING of no responsibilities (when I'd poked my head in the guestroom to tell Matthew I had to run out, he and the two dogs were asleep), I drove round a while to cool off. I pulled over at a pretty little spot and drank in the long vista of smoky mountains, the blue sky fighting to hold its own through the haze.

It wasn't lost on me that while Matthew was trying to get his memory back, I felt plagued by memories I wanted to forget. Like all those things of mine that Fiona took without asking. She'd sent some muscle guys from the hospital that day I was off making a furniture delivery, and she musta given them an awful long list. When I got home, I was knocked back on my heels.

All I could figure was she'd sent that box of junk to remind me how small my world was—holding on to such pathetic shards of a life. Like I was thinking I'd better never get rid of anything since nothing good was ever gonna come my way. My face felt as though she'd reached out and slapped me, but really it was my own shame creeping up my neck, making my cheeks burn.

As I drove away fast, I kicked up an awful cloud of dust and rocks hit the back of the truck. Who cared? What was one more dent? When I got to the highway, my mind started playing tricks, working hard to convince me that she was really trying to connect with me. Why else would she bother to drag a heavy box to the post office and pay all that money? But before long that notion fell by the wayside. If that had been the truth, she'd've tucked a jar of marmalade inside or a packet of my favorite Irish sweets. Or even just signed the note. No, she was saying good riddance to bad rubbish.

BY THE TIME I got home, it was well past our usual suppertime. I'd been hoping Matthew had started something, but he and those blame dogs were still in bed.

"Huh? Oh, yeah, hi, Abit. Sorry. We fell asleep," he said, rubbing his eyes. Mollie had the nerve to yawn real big. "Best sleep I've had in ages."

"Well, lucky you. I'm glad someone round here is sleeping good—besides those dogs." I called Mollie, and of course her new buddy followed. I got them fed and started making our supper. I fried up some chicken, pulled together coleslaw, and found leftover biscuits to warm. I put the coffee on to perk.

Afterwards, when I'd finished my second cup, I excused myself to spend time in the woodshop. Matthew asked if I needed help, but what I needed was time on my own.

I especially enjoyed the woodshop of a summer's evening. The light from the late-setting sun and the music of the crickets set against the quiet of dusk made it feel special. And something about the scent of a day's worth of sawdust and linseed oil fueled my creativity. But not that night. After a day like that one, I was just trying to work through thoughts of being a no count. I turned my anger inwards, mad at myself for letting Fiona in long enough to set off another world of hurt.

I stared at an order I'd started but had been putting off. I ragged at myself for not getting to it, but I knew why. It was for a table like the one that doctor had ordered for Fiona, way back before we'd married, the first time she'd dumped me. I reminded myself I needed the money, so I picked up some wood and started to turn one of the legs. I got some satisfaction from the strength of the wood and the power of the chisel as the leg took shape. But when I set it down and started on the next leg, a wave of grief came roaring in, surprising me oncet again. I tried to fend off the raw feelings, but I failed against their strong tide and started to cry. I carried on that way for some time. Until.

A hand pressed against my back offering gentle comfort, and my hurt just fell away. It felt so good that for a precious moment I thought it was the hand of Jesus consoling me. After a time, though, I knew it had to be Matthew. While I woulda preferred Jesus, it was a fine thing to have a friend.

Chapter 17
Della

"HONEY, HOW ARE YOU DOING?" I asked when Abit answered his phone. I hadn't heard from him lately and wanted to know how things were going on the farm.

"Oh, I'm much better now. Something happened to set me back, but I'm okay," he said, answering my concerns before I shared them. We were old friends and had some kind of telepathy going between us. "What about you and Alex? Have you come up with anything?"

"Sorry to report that we're stumped. No wait. That's too definitive. I should say *not yet*. We're still searching. It's got me thinking about that club Nigel had back in England. I wished we'd formed one. You know, calling on our friends' and neighbors' expertise when a case required it."

"Maybe, but that club brought a lot of heartache too. Besides, don't you remember, not long after we got home, you tried. Johnny Richards is good at splitting wood, and Mrs.

Dougherty makes a fine onion marmalade, but we hadn't any call for that kind of expertise."

I had to laugh. "You're right. I don't suppose we have the right friends. Present company excluded."

We chatted a while longer and came up with a new plan. When I hung up, I went back to see how Alex was doing with the church and French-teacher leads. It wasn't that he'd given up—just that so many results showed up, he was having to painstakingly wade through lengthy lists. We both wished we could ask for some official help from law enforcement, but it was too early to get Sheriff Aaron Horne involved. One, he was lazy, so I needed more facts to whet his appetite. Two, I had to (reluctantly) honor Matthew's wish to learn more about himself before being subjected to public—and police—scrutiny. But I *could* ask Horne about the body found in the wilderness. It was hard to imagine that wasn't related to Matthew's predicament. The timing was spot on.

That would have to wait, though. Abit and I had agreed to head to Asheville the next day to explore some of the swanker men's stores. It was a longshot, but they might recognize the blue handkerchief. The fabric was exquisite, at least where there wasn't blood. We'd folded it in a way that hid the shock of the ugly stain.

After I saw Abit pull up at Coburn's the next morning, I headed down the steps of my apartment. I left Rascal with Alex; that dog always thought he wanted to go with me, but then whined and carried on in the car when I went in somewhere that didn't allow dogs. When I reached the parking lot, I couldn't find Abit. I looked inside Coburn's front window and saw him talking with Annie. I knocked on the window and headed to the Jeep.

Abit and I had enjoyed some fine road trips over the years. Washington, D.C.; Atherton, Virginia; even the short jaunts up to Boone, N.C., to name a few. They usually involved some kind of detective work, and I hoped this trip was as successful as those had been. And while I was wishing, how about less dangerous?

"Takes you back, doesn't it?" Abit said once we were out of Laurel Falls.

"I was just thinking the same thing."

"I've missed our trips. But, of course, I've had a family to rear."

"You still do, Honey."

"Doesn't feel that way."

As we approached Asheville, I pulled off I-40 and turned east on Tunnel Road.

"I thought we were going downtown," Abit said.

"And I thought you'd like to stop at your favorite restaurant before we got too deep into this caper." He slapped his thigh and laughed. Traffic was always a surprise after Laurel Falls, but we hit a series of well-coordinated traffic lights and pulled into the parking lot for Lulu's Café.

I always marveled at—and envied—what Abit could pack away. I had a similar appetite, but not the metabolism. I'd be as big as Old Man Clendenin if I'd ordered the way Abit did: baked chicken, yellow squash casserole, green beans, buttermilk biscuits *and* cornbread, peach cobbler.

We waddled out and even after a couple cups of good, strong coffee, I wanted to nap way more than I wanted to detect. But I shook that off as we approached the front door of Britches. The thick scent of aftershave or room freshener struck me as the front door closed behind us. Probably some formula that promised to make customers buy more, though it would have sent me back to the car if we hadn't been on a mission. Even though only a couple of customers wandered the store, the handsome young clerk acted too busy to help. (Admittedly, we didn't look like good prospects for his commission.) He did a nice job of filling out his custom-tailored suit, and the boutonniere was a classy touch, but they couldn't make up for his lousy attitude. He seemed bored when we showed him the handkerchief inside the plastic bag. No, they didn't sell *hankies*, he'd said with a sneer. Whatever happened to curiosity, let alone courtesy?

We were walking down Biltmore Avenue toward The Men's Store when Abit said, "I almost started laughing at that guy, acting all rich-like, talking in a soft, faky voice. Unless his daddy owns the store, he's likely pulling in eight dollars an hour in a town that would eat that up before the middle of the month. I don't know where people earning minimum wage get the idea they can act snooty. Don't get me wrong. I'm not knocking their wages—I doubt I even make that much—but just because they cater to wealthy folks doesn't give them the right to act thataway."

"If they earned a million dollars it doesn't give them the right," I said. "Let's hope this next one has nicer staff. Otherwise, we'll need to find other stores in the area." I sighed and added, "I wish we could just show them a picture of Matthew and get this over with."

"Don't have one," Abit said as he opened the front door of The Men's Store. "And besides, we promised not to give him away before he was ready."

My spirits perked up when Mr. Porter, according to his brass nametag, looked at our blue handkerchief and said, "Yes, this is one of ours. Lovely silk fabric, isn't it?" He was dressed much like Mr. Britches, but sported a more generous disposition. "Let me take it out of the bag just to be sure so I can ..."

"Er, no, that's okay," Abit said, snatching it away. We couldn't let him see the blood. I supposed we could have claimed a bloody nose, but still, we wanted to spare him that sight. "Can you tell us anything about who might have bought it?"

"Oh, how exciting. This sounds like something I saw on CSI. Are you detectives?"

Hey, our lucky day. He was into this. It seemed to go that way—either people enjoyed being part of the chase or looked down on us. We didn't say anything and in time, he went on. "We maintain excellent records of who buys what. We keep track of all our bespoke suits and shirts, of course, as well as measurements and personal information. Gives us an opportunity to cross-sell and thank them accordingly at the holidays."

"Any chance we could get the names of those handkerchief customers? It really is a case of life or death." I knew I was piling it on, but we needed that list.

"Uh, I'm afraid not. We offer our patrons the strictest confidentiality."

"Well, it's not like you're lawyers or doctors," I said. I didn't want to antagonize him, but we'd driven over an hour on windy roads to get here.

"No, absolutely not." He looked perturbed with me, and I couldn't blame him. But I couldn't let this go, either. Fortunately, the hundred dollar bill I slid across the glass counter turned his frown upside down. Just then the bell over the door chimed. He did a little finger wave and kept the smile plastered across his face. In a hushed tone, he said, "Go get a coffee next door and come back in fifteen." Just like on TV.

Abit was beside himself when we settled into a booth at Pour Folks, the café Mr. Porter suggested. "I can't believe you walk round with hundred dollar bills in your purse. And how did you pull that out like a magician, all folded just right?"

"Old habits."

"Mr. Porter is in for a good time tonight, but I hate to see you throw your money away like that on somebody else's problems."

"Oh, it felt so good, it was worth every penny. Now we'll have more names to match against those Alex is already working on."

"What if someone bought that hanky for him? A gift?"

"Hmm. I hadn't thought of that. But something tells me Matthew's bought a few 'bespoke suits' in that very shop."

"What does 'bespoke' mean, anyways?"

"Custom made."

"Why don't just they say that?"

"Likely for the same reason you say 'reckon' instead of 'guess.'" I looked at my watch and added, "Drink up, we need to head home." He just sat there. I could tell he had something on his mind, but he was struggling to get the words out. "Come on, Abit. Spit it out."

"Could we swing by Fiona's on the way out of town?" He looked pitiful, like a teenager spying on a girlfriend who'd been flirting with someone else.

"Sure, Honey. I should have thought of that myself. Of course you want to know where your boys are staying when they're down here. And, hey, nothing wrong with knowing where she's landed."

After we snared the list from Mr. Porter, I drove across the bridge to West Asheville, twisting around some curvy roads to 80 Kansas Avenue. The neighborhood streets all seemed to have state names. I pulled over at the intersection with Nebraska Avenue. I'd done enough surveillance back in the day to do it right. Abit sunk down in the passenger seat.

"The boys are outside. Take a peek."

They were playing with some sticks in the front yard, just horsing around. They seemed a little old for that, but maybe there wasn't much else for them to do in such a small yard. I was glad Fiona wasn't outside with them. Abit could take his time watching them in all their boyishness. Pretty soon, though, we saw a screen door open, and they ran inside.

Abit sat back up. "Typical. Fiona ruining my fun oncet again."

Chapter 18
Abit

THE NEXT DAY IN THE WOODSHOP, I told Matthew about our trip to Asheville. I was hoping something like Lulu's or Britches might ring a bell. I saw his eyes flare when I mentioned The Men's Store, but otherwise he was still as a post. I felt weary from all the mystery.

"I know it seems we're not making much progress," Matthew said, reading my mind again, "but step back a moment. We now know I'm a Gallophile (*What in the world was that? I thought. A wine drinker?*), I must reside in Asheville, and I more than likely buy fine clothing and handkerchiefs. Though we don't know for certain the latter is mine."

"*Yet*. Alex is working on it now. And it's just too much of a coincidence that a bloody handkerchief made of silk happens to land in the wilderness near my farm. What else do we know?"

"Something I think about every day. You saved my life."

"Oh, I wouldn't take it that far."

"I would. I was face down in your creek. Spent. If you hadn't come along ..."

"Okay, I see your point, but don't make it out to be so heroic. I just did what any decent human being would do."

"Perhaps." He nodded slightly and went back to sanding. After a while, he slipped out, likely to make our midday dinner. It was an understatement to say I was enjoying his cookery services. And soon enough I was chomping into a big club sandwich filled with leftover bacon and cheese, tomato, and lettuce between toasted bread, all held together with a toothpick. We were drinking coffee afterwards when he said, "Tell me about your past. At least one of us has one."

"Oh, you don't want mine. *I* don't want mine. I've had some hardships."

"Yes, I'm sure you have. It shows around your eyes. But look at where you are now. You're a self-made man."

"Oh, no, I wouldn't've made someone like me."

"Stop that, Abit. You're running on an old script. Take a look at your life. You're a successful woodworker. You play mandolin in a bluegrass band. You own a farm people would give their right arm to own. You have a family of three, four counting Mollie."

"Okay. I've had some luck too. At The Hicks, thanks to Alex Covington who got me a scholarship and paid some of my expenses, I got to talk with counselors who explained how I wouldn't be *me* without that stinking childhood. At first I thought that sounded like claptrap, but then it sunk in what they meant. I've accepted that my past is just what it is. Was."

"You're sounding better all the time. Now start living that and get rid of those old messages."

"Like you did?"

He sat silent for the longest time. "I hadn't thought about my situation in that light, but, yes, you could be right."

"I reckon we both needed to lose our old thinking. You did it in a grand style. I was making progress in that direction, but Fiona's leaving turned me backwards."

By then we were doing the dishes, and we both stopped to listen. A truck was making its way toward the house. Matthew stared hard at me—like I had any control over who used my drive. I went out, wiping my hands on a towel, and the dogs started up, running alongside a Chevy pickup so covered in Bondo it was hard to make out what color it was.

When the truck stopped, I let out a laugh. "Duane Dockery. What brings you to Hanging Dog?" I asked through his rolled-down window. I hadn't seen him since he and his wife, Mary Lou, picked up stakes and moved away. Given what we'd learned about Mary Lou and what she'd been up to, I was surprised he was showing his face round these parts.

"I've moved back, Abit, and I need a place to stay."

Man, why are all these folks showing up now? I grumbled to myself. But Duane had been my best friend for years, back when I was a boy and we took the Rollin' Store all round the county.

I motioned for him to park over by the barn. When he got outta the truck, I gave him a big hug. Best I could recall, it had been Mary Lou who'd caused all the trouble, not Duane. He was just a loyal husband. Or henpecked. I explained to him about the guestroom and how he could have the boys' room instead. He grabbed his grip, and we headed inside. I hoped Matthew would lay low for now.

I left Duane to settle in and put fresh sheets on the bed himself; I hadn't changed them since Curtis left. I eased outta the house to find Matthew, who was hiding in the guestroom. I could see him standing at the window, curtain pulled back, watching the house like a nosy neighbor. When I went inside without knocking, I said, "He's my old friend, Matthew." He still looked angry, so I added, "This is my home, you know."

"But you said ..."

"Yeah, I know what I said about no one coming here, and for the better part of a year, no one did. So what? Oncet you got here I'm supposed to close the gate? After what's been happening, I'm not making any promises about who might or might not come. I don't expect to hear any more about it. We're working round it."

He had a startled look on his face. I probably did too.

Turned out Duane and Matthew kinda hit it off. In his spare time, Matthew had come up with a story about his past, so he could answer basic questions: Where are you from? *Oh, I started out in Asheville, but I've been trying out different places.* What did you do before? *I taught some and did some woodworking.* Any of your people from round here? *No, just my new friend, Abit.* Things like that. I could see how he'd woven together some of what we talked about like Asheville and teaching. For a while longer, his secrets were safe.

Chapter 19
Abit

DUANE HEADED OUT TO LOOK for work the next morning, and I told Matthew I had some errands to run. I did, but really I just wanted to go somewhere normal. Where people were doing ordinary things. Shopping, gassing up their truck, buying a sandwich from Adam's Rib.

I did all those things, finishing up by ordering a barbecued chicken sandwich to go from The Rib, as locals called it. Then I drove Mollie and me to a nearby park for a makeshift picnic. Not the wilderness kind of park, but the family kind with picnic tables and jungle gym stuff for kids and trails that led off from there. As I walked toward a trailhead, I came upon a bench with a memorial plaque the way people do when someone's passed. I read the inscription: "We are grateful for every minute together." I was surprised to read it was for a child, a boy who hadn't even made it to 4 year old. I sat on the bench and saw how it was positioned in a pretty little spot, lined up with a ridgeline that would offer a beautiful sunset of an evening. I imagined the family here together, happy, enjoying a picnic on a blanket, the little boy dancing round the way children do, more aware than older folks of the specialness that surrounded them. Until.

I got Mollie up on the bench (I knew the boy would approve) and ate my sandwich. After I gave my crusts to her, we sat quiet-like for some time. A soft summer breeze blew past me, carrying the scent of something blooming nearby, sweet and hopeful. And of course I thought about my boys. I'd been more than grateful for them both, and because I'd been able to work from home, we'd spent a lot of time together. But I vowed to give them even more from now on. And to get my life together.

When I got back in the truck, I turned on the radio. Reception was bad out that way, but I could just make out some country music playing. About halfway home, the news came on. I turned it up—I'd felt out of touch with what was going on beyond my driveway. The first story was about a bruhaha at the county commissioners' meeting, followed by a report on the sale of some county land. I started feeling kinda dozy but jolted awake when the announcer said the body found in the wilderness had been identified as a drug dealer from Asheville. Law enforcement (I was sure that meant Curtis and the FBI) already had him on their watch lists. The announcer went on about "significant leads" as to who the killer was.

I couldn't concentrate on the road after that and had to pull the truck over, my stomach churning and my mind racing. *Was Matthew that killer? Was he like Clive Ownbey, nice on the outside, rotten on the inside? Maybe he was the kingpin, angry that this dealer was cheating him outta money. Hadn't Matthew flashed on having wealth? Drugs sure were a fast way to get ahold of a lot of money. He didn't seem to have a habit of his own, but then those kingpins, at least on TV, never did. They just wreaked their havoc on folks until they made them poor—in body, spirit, and pocketbook. What kind of a wild man had I let into my home?*

I carried on like that for a while, until a feeling came over me that can only be described as a terrible joy. Something awful had happened, but it offered a way to the truth. That body had been found, the feds were on the case, and finally a resolution to this mystery was in the works.

As I drove by a hardware store on the way home, I pulled in. A few evenings ago when Matthew was having one of his ups and downs, he asked for a birdfeeder. "If I have to be stuck in this room while that convoy of friends and acquaintances come up here, I'd like to have something nice to look at." At the time, I thought he was stepping outta line, but now I could see his point.

Oncet back home, I carried the feeder straight to the guestroom. When I knocked, he kinda grumbled to come in. Both dogs were in there, lying on the bed with him, and I felt like an intruder in my own home. But when Matthew saw the birdfeeder, he looked as happy as I'd ever seen him. I found a hook, and we got it all set up. "You can fill it from that big sack of seed in my shop," I told him. He looked kinda sheepish, like he'd probably been lying in bed reading me the riot act. I figured that was a good time to tell him we needed to go back to the wilderness. I tried to act all confident-like, but I heard a catch in my voice. I was nervous talking to someone who could be a killer, and he saw right through me.

"Listen, Abit. I know I could be a dangerous person, but look at me." He held his arms out straight and kinda posed. "I just don't think so. Wouldn't I have some sense of being that awful? And aren't you the one who told me to look on the bright side? I could be heir to a fortune, I believe you phrased it. Maybe I'm a good guy, the victim in all this." He paused and added, "And yes, let's go to the wilderness, as long as we stay clear of the FBI."

I FIGURED WE NEEDED to drive this time, so I got out my map with all the parking places near wilderness trailheads. That had to be what the killer had done—driven to remote places where he could dump the bodies with little chance of

being seen. These trails really are in the middle
of nowhere, especially on a weekday.

We didn't say much as I headed to the parking
area closest to where the drug dealer was found.
When we drove up, a small group of lawmen
still hung round, but the parking lot had been
reopened to the public. They had guards all
over where they'd roped it off with yellow crime
tape, so we skirted that and acted like we were
just fixing to hike. Matthew pulled his hat low
and ambled off ahead of me. I was glad he didn't
act all guilty-like.

We hiked a bit and circled round to see the
crime area from a different direction. It was a
hot day, the sun burning the sky 'til it'd turned
white hot, not a lick of blue. When we came to
an opening with a small lake, the water looked
scorched from the rays of the strong summer
sun.

As we sat under some trees, I looked up. A
kaleidoscope of light and shapes played out as
the sun winked through treetops swaying in the
soft breeze. It made me light-headed, prayerful
even, as though I'd tapped into the celestial
realm. Maybe I had. Or maybe I just needed to
eat something.

I'd made a coupla cheese sandwiches and
brought some cookies I'd bought at Coburn's.
Not much of a supper, but we could snack when
we got home. As I set the sandwiches on a
nearby log, Matthew suddenly jumped up and
ran all round it. I didn't think this spread was

worth that kind of excitement, but then I saw why he was carrying on. I nearly died laughing.

"What?" he said, swatting at something in front of his face. "It's not funny, Abit. Something is after me."

"It's just a News Bee." I laughed some more, though to be fair, when I was a kid, they worried me sick 'til Mama told me about them. They are the meanest looking hornet you can imagine, getting to well over an inch in size. And they hover in front of your face making the loudest racket. But that's the thing: It's all for show. They don't have a stinger. Carrying on like that is how they protect themselves in the natural world.

Matthew was kinda glaring at me, but I patted the log to get him to sit down again so I could explain. Oncet he caught his breath, I told him the News Bee is known for bringing good news.

"Well, we could sure use some."

After a bit, I asked, "Anything today seem familiar?"

"Not a thing. Including that flying varmint."

I chuckled. And that *was* good news, in a way. At least he didn't remember dumping the drug dealer nearby. But that wasn't strong enough to prove he wasn't involved. When we got up to walk back to the truck, I noticed Matthew kinda dragged his feet. I wasn't the only one weary of all this mess.

But looking at that parking lot, something finally dawned on me. If Matthew were the killer, where had he stashed *his* car? He'd've had to park it before he dumped the drug dealer, and then how or why did he, Matthew, get beat up and have to crawl along my creek? I know a lot of things coulda happened in between—like an accomplice clobbered him and took off—but I hung my hopes on my latest notion.

As we got to my truck, some loud-mouth kids came running past us. Probably out doing a looky-loo at the crime scene. "Here now, walk, don't run," Matthew said to them. One of the guys gave him the finger, and they laughed as they ran on.

Well, that did it. There was no question in my mind Matthew was a teacher. They must say those words a hundred times a day. I sure heard them, even just that short time I was in regular school. I knew it wasn't funny, but I couldn't help but laugh. Matthew got a confused look on his face.

"I'm sorry, but you sounded like every teacher in the world."

He waved his hand, like what I'd just said was a given. "No, it's not that. I just had a flash. I saw a smart-alecky kid, back at a school of some kind, giving me the finger, the same way that boy did."

"Well, that doesn't narrow things down much. If you counted up how many fingers were given at schools on any day, all over this state, it would take a calculator to add them all up."

Matthew smiled. "I think you're right. I believe I've seen them many times before, as though I had eyes in the back of my head."

"Let's get back so I can call Della. They can add that finger flash to their research."

Chapter 20
Della

ALEX HAD HIS NOSE in the computer when I told him I was heading to Newland to try to pull information out of Sheriff Horne. He looked up, his eyes bleary. "I'm narrowing things down, Della. That list of twenty-nine customers from The Men's Store is now only six likely candidates. Later this morning, I want to cross-reference that with the list of French teachers and professors in Western North Carolina. It's just that I've got a fire to put out for the magazine first."

I hated to pile on, but I had to ask. "Any luck with the red door at 1247 somewhere or other?"

"That's another long list. I was able to finetune it by looking only in zip codes where the upper-crust live. Based on what you said about Matthew's demeanor and clothing, I think that's a good direction. But then I remembered Episcopal churches usually have red doors, so the list grew again—though I doubt they have brass numerals on them. Except Matthew's memories can't be taken literally; he may have combined images in his mind." He sighed and drank some cold coffee. "See what I'm up against?"

I gave him a hug and left.

I KNEW THE BEST WAY to grab Horne's attention was the promise of caffeine and sugar. As I walked into his office, I noticed he already had crumbs on his tie. He stood and brushed those off to make room for a new crop. We walked down the street to Cookie's, where he ordered two doughnuts—raspberry jelly and chocolate covered—plus a large coffee. I got a brownie and a latte.

"So, what's this bribery about?" he said, his hands motioning across our table.

When I'd first met Horne in 1994, he didn't need bribes; he was excited about his work. But over the years, he'd gotten lazier, a trend I'd seen in other sheriffs and lawmen. It didn't help that early on in his tenure he'd overheard some locals imitating him. I was there that day, outside the store, when they were doing a darned good job of it. Horne had a booming voice, and his first name of Aaron had earned him the nickname Air, as in Airhorn. We were all surprised when he walked up. His face turned a deep shade of magenta, fueled by anger and humiliation. From then on, his attitude kept slipping. Add to that the fact that his job was comprised mostly of tedious parking tickets, jaywalkers, and the occasional domestic dispute. Together they vanquished any idealism he'd brought to the job.

"Well, I've been wondering what was happening with the body found in the wilderness."

"Decomposition, I reckon," he said, spraying confectioner's sugar onto my black blouse as he bit into the jelly doughnut.

"Oh, come on, Horne. We've done some good work together. Give me *something*."

He chewed a while longer, relishing my tension before saying, "Seems that guy was a drug dealer—mostly meth—with a rap sheet longer than the list of people I'd love to lock up—not all of them criminals. So it appears another druggie scum is off the streets. End of case."

"Seriously? No more investigation? And for the record, that was already on the news, so you still owe me."

"Given all the cutbacks, we don't have the manpower to delve into drug-related deaths, especially when the phrase 'good riddance' is on the tip of every investigator's tongue." I thought he was using *we* rather royally, knowing the FBI wasn't as indolent as his sheriff's department. But I didn't want to rile him, so I kept my mouth shut. "Man, these doughnuts are good," he said, as though that was ever in question.

"Tell me something I don't know."

He laughed before chomping down on the chocolate-iced one. "Okay, he was killed by a gunshot to the gut. Bled out somewhere else, then dumped in the wilderness. Nothing to write home about."

"What's his name?" I asked, determined to get my money's worth.

He smiled and held up a finger. "Ah, I remember that because his first name is my brother-in-law's, and his last is my mother's maiden name. Roger Ledbetter."

I finally had something worth writing in my old reporter's notebook. It must have been 25 years old, edges slightly curled and yellowed, but it felt great in my hand.

Chapter 21
Abit

THE NEXT TRUCK IN THE CARAVAN up my drive belonged to Owen Kent from the Rollin' Ramblers. He stopped by to ask if I felt up to performing at the concert scheduled for Friday night. It was at a favorite venue—just over the county line in a remodeled barn with weathered wood walls and a high ceiling that made for nearabout perfect acoustics. I'd completely forgotten about the gig, which Owen picked up on. He seemed kinda embarrassed—for *me*. I could only hope, for his sake, he'd never let his life go so low.

He handed me the set list, and I looked it over while he got his guitar outta the truck. We had a good practice session, right there in the yard, with Matthew not far off in his room and Duane barreling back up the drive when his workday was over. I didn't have any privacy anymore. But if I was gonna play in front of hundreds of people, I needed to get used to performing again. I appreciated Owen's kindness in bringing me back into the fold.

THE NIGHT OF THE CONCERT, Duane and Matthew piled into the front seat of my truck. It was pretty tight, but fortunately none of us were wide in the hips. We left the dogs inside the guestroom so they wouldn't run down the road, trying to follow us. I figured if they got up to no good, the damage in there would be less than in the house.

It had taken some convincing to get Matthew to join us. This would be his first time offa the farm since he'd arrived. But with that beard and the clothes he was wearing, I couldn't imagine anyone would recognize him from before, whatever that was. Duane, of course, didn't know anything about Matthew's situation, so we had to talk about it in the guestroom. After some fast talking on my part, Matthew finally agreed.

To help with his disguise, I gave him a red bandana and some fake glasses from one of the boy's Halloween costumes. Even I barely recognized him when he met up with Duane and me at the truck. To be honest, he looked a little strange, all covered up with a hat and bandana and his vest, especially given it was summertime. Fortunately the hot spell had passed; otherwise he woulda suffocated in all that gear. And he could count on people round here giving strange plenty of room. Sure, they'd gossip and talk about it, make fun even, but in the end, there's a strong sense of live and let live. It's like if it's here, it's ours, so that's okay. But if those same people were to read about it happening, say, in Charlotte or Washington, D.C., well, that would be an almighty disgrace. It's odd, but it kinda works, at least locally.

When we pulled up at the venue, I could tell Matthew was scared to get outta the truck. Duane looked at him funny, then glanced my way for guidance. I just shrugged, grabbed my mando, and went to find the rest of the band.

It felt good to see all the Rollin' Ramblers in one place, and they greeted me like an old friend. The barn was just as I'd remembered: wood everywhere, sawdust on the floor, a hint of its former life perfuming the air. When we came out on stage, I could see Matthew and Duane sitting in the back, and truth be known, Matthew didn't look any more peculiar than the rest of the crowd.

We played "Redhaired Boy" and "Foggy Mountain Special," which I knew the band had chosen as a welcome back, being they were two of my favorites. I saw Matthew tapping his toes to the music, even though I had a strong sense it wasn't his kinda music. I'd've placed a bet on Mozart and Puccini.

While Luther Blake played a break on his banjo, I kept watch over the crowd and noticed a few people staring over Matthew's way, but mostly it seemed to be middle-aged women who musta thought he looked like a new prospect.

After the concert, Duane attracted plenty of attention of his own. People gave him the benefit of the doubt—I reckoned they figured he'd been led on by his crazy wife—and offered up howdies like nothing had happened. Everything was working out fine—until we were walking to the truck.

"Excuse me," someone called out. We acted like we thought they were calling to somebody else and quickened our pace. Somehow Duane knew just what to do, or was good at following my lead.

"Excuse me," the voice said again, reaching out and taking hold of Matthew's sleeve. I knew he wanted to swat at her—by now I could tell it was a woman—but he just stopped and stared at her through those glasses. "You look so familiar," she said. "Have we met?"

I almost busted out laughing. Even I knew that was one of the oldest pickup lines in the book. But Matthew didn't seem to know—or didn't remember—and he just shook his head. "Not likely," he mumbled.

"Uh, he's just passing through," I added, not sure if that helped or not.

She took his hand and shook it, gentle like and said she hoped to see him round.

We were all laughing and teasing Matthew. Then Duane saw a beer vendor who was taking advantage of thirsty customers as they left the show. He and Matthew veered off to the stand; I was driving, so I kept walking toward the truck. I waited what felt like forever. By the time they got back, I didn't feel much like driving, but Duane was still drinking and Matthew wasn't about to get behind the wheel of my truck.

No one said a thing on the way home, which was a shame, because I was pleased with the way I'd played. I guessed some things don't leave you altogether. And that mando was a fine instrument, the kind that makes you sound better than you deserve.

As I drove, Duane seemed to get more riled up from his drinking. By the time we piled outta the truck, he started teasing Matthew about something. Turned out, Matthew had a slip of paper with that woman's phone number on it. She'd shoved it into his hand when she shook it. I joined in the teasing, but not too hard. I could tell he was kinda pleased.

It wasn't 'til Duane had gone on to his room in the house and we'd let the dogs out (they were sleeping on the bed and hadn't chewed a thing) that I asked the familiar question. "Did the music or venue bring back any memories?" I wasn't holding out for anything, so I was surprised when he said yes.

"Don't take this personally, because I really enjoyed your music, but as I sat there, I flashed on a concert in a small hall, about the size of that barn. Only it was rather rococo—all filigreed and trimmed with gold. And they were playing

Mozart. Not all that well, mind you. They looked so very young. Perhaps students."

"I knew it. You're some kind of teacher or principal or something like that," I said. Matthew got that look again—both happy and scared. Then I added, "I'm gonna tell Alex to keep checking schools in Asheville. And if that room you imagined is as fancy as you said, it must be at a private school. That should cut the research time in half. We're getting closer."

Chapter 22
Della

WHEN I GOT BACK to the store, Annie was talking with an older woman. From their body language, I could tell Granny was making a fuss. Probably didn't like so much orange peel in her marmalade or garlic in her pasta sauce. We got a lot of that.

Annie looked relieved to see me, eager to turn the situation over. "Della, this woman wants to put up a poster."

"That's fine. We've got room on the bulletin board." We'd already posted several notices publicizing a local quilt auction and a fundraiser for someone in the community who needed surgery.

"Well, it's not the usual ..." Annie said, her voice trailing off.

Granny turned to me and said in a harsh voice, "Looky here, this is serious. We need the community's help. The sheriff sent me."

"Oh, he did, did he? He usually brings things like this himself." She had no idea I'd just come from my meeting with Horne, who hadn't mentioned deputizing Ma Barker.

"Well, he's really busy and this is important, so he asked some of us to help out."

Now I really knew she was lying. "Like a posse?" I asked.

"Yeah. Kinda."

"Okay, let me have a closer look at this important document," I said, unable to keep the sarcasm out of my voice. As I unrolled the poster, I lost my voice completely when I stared at Matthew's face looking out at me below the headline: HAVE YOU SEEN THIS MAN?

I swallowed hard and rerolled the poster, mostly to stall for time. "I'll put this up later today. I'm awfully busy right now."

"I could just tape it in your window."

"Oh, no. No one even looks in the windows anymore—they're more likely to notice things like this when I put them on the bulletin board, as I mentioned earlier." Come on, Granny. This is *my* store.

"Well, if you promise."

"Leave it with me. I'll get to it, I promise," I said, crossing my heart with my index finger.

Yeah, I promise all right. I promise to take it out to show Abit and Matthew.

Chapter 23
Abit

DELLA'S JEEP CAME FLYING up the driveway. I figured if this kept up, I'd need to gravel a parking lot at the top of the hill. Duane had found him a place to stay, so at least he wasn't parked in the way. And Matthew had taken the dogs to his room, hiding after we both heard the grinding gears.

I was smiling, happy to see Della, but she had a terrible expression on her face when she got outta the car. She looked round, like she was worried who else was there. "Where is he?" she growled, kinda whispering.

"What's up?"

"This." She unrolled a poster. It took my brain a few moments to get things straight. Matthew was staring out at me, wearing a coat and tie, and his hair—all trimmed and combed—didn't look like it did now, but it was definitely Matthew. "What's all this about? How'd you get this?" I asked, my throat gone dry.

"Can we go somewhere safe to talk?"

I knew she was just protecting me, but it ticked me off she didn't think I had sense enough to know right from wrong. Other than his occasional ups and downs, Matthew hadn't given me anything to worry about, and I'd finally made my peace with him.

When I told her that, she grabbed my arm and pulled me toward the house. We went in through the kitchen, and she musta smelled coffee on the stove because she asked for a cup. I was pouring her one when she said, "Look, I know you like this guy, but he doesn't remember who he is. He could be a reincarnated Al Capone or Ted Bundy for all we know."

She was starting to scare me. I read the rest of the poster, but it just sounded like family or friends trying to find a loved one. "This doesn't make him out to be a criminal, Della."

"Well, of course not. The FBI wouldn't send Granny to put up a wanted poster in Coburn's. That's how I got ahold of this. But her story was all mixed up. When I asked a few questions, she got rattled and said in that impatient way country women have, 'Well, are you gonna put this blamed thing in your window or not?' I told her I'd post it on the bulletin board—but I didn't tell her when."

"We need to show this to Matthew."

"But he won't remember. Or do you think he's faking?"

"I'm not faking, Ms. Kincaid." Matthew had come in through the front door so quiet-like we hadn't heard him.

"Okay, maybe I'm too suspicious, Matthew," Della said. "I like you. Abit likes you. Mollie likes you, though that's not much of a qualifier. But I'm sure you can understand that we know nothing about you, *you* know nothing about you, and when people start coming into my store with something that's only one degree away from a wanted poster, I can't help but worry about Abit out here alone with you."

He turned and nearabout ran outta the kitchen. I hollered after him to stay so we could talk it through and come up with a plan, but he just let the screen door slam behind him.

"See what I mean, Abit?"

"Oh, shut up, Della."

We were both so surprised by what I'd said that we stopped and stared at each other for the longest time. Then I started to laugh. Not a mirthful one, more like exasperation and fatigue catching up with me. "I'm sorry, but you've got to give me a little more credit. I've been living with this guy for weeks now, and I just don't think he's dangerous."

Della didn't say anything. I was squirming in my chair, begging for this moment to pass. It did when she quickly rolled up the poster and turned to go. Then, just as sudden-like, she sat back down. Her face changed, and I thought she was about to start in again on Matthew. Instead she began to cry. I just stood there at first, but then I stepped over to be next to her. When she calmed down, she squeezed my hand. "Oh, Honey, I was so scared for you. I know I overstepped. *Again*. But please be careful."

"I will," I said. "And you too. I don't like these folks coming into your store. I don't suppose you got her name did you?"

"Hey, I may not have been a reporter for some time, but I haven't lost the touch. Her name is Imogene Caruthers. Alex is working on her story as we speak."

Chapter 24
Abit

AFTER DELLA LEFT, I just sat on the porch swing, like I was waiting for something. Not sure what. The boys to come home? Oh, sure, those thoughts flowed through me as steady as our creek down below. No, this was different. It took a while, but then I knew. For the other shoe to drop.

I headed out to the barn to talk with Matthew. Of course he wouldn't open up. "Come on, Matthew. Open the door. It's my barn!" I was getting tired of all these folks running in and out of my home, treating me like some butler opening and closing doors for them. Just one month ago no one but me and Mollie roamed this hill.

"Listen, Matthew, I'm sorry about all that," I said through the door, "but you've got to see it from Della's view. She and Alex are spending their time—for free, I might add—to figure out who in the world you are. Not to put you behind bars but to help you find yourself again."

I heard the lock turn.

He barely cracked the door, then turned away and lay down on his bed. The dogs didn't even bother to say hello before they flew past me and ran outside. I settled on the chair and waited. Finally he said, "That poster freaked me out. It wasn't Della. I know she and her husband or ex-husband or whoever he is are helping. But with a poster like that out and about, it's only a matter of time before I'm caught."

I didn't like the way he used that word *caught*. "What do you mean by that? Are you remembering something that could get you *caught*?" My heart pounded so hard that last word came out funny.

"No, nothing like that," he said, wiping his forehead and getting his long hair outta his face. "Just that I can feel law enforcement closing in, and I'm an easy target. I can't even defend myself." He paused before adding, "And I've got this terrible feeling I must be guilty of a heinous crime."

"Why?
Earlier you said you'd be able to sense if you were that awful. What's changed?"

"That was just happy talk, Abit. I was in danger of dying when you saved me. You don't get in that condition without something serious happening."

"They coulda done something mean to you first. And Della just told me some old woman was taking the posters round the town. I don't get it either—you're likely from Asheville, so what is she doing with that poster up *here*? Besides, no one has seen you."

"That postman did. And don't they have wanted posters in every post office?"

"That wasn't exactly a wanted poster, and I doubt you're one of the ten most wanted." I was trying for a joke, but then I realized none of us knew Matthew *wasn't* one of the ten most wanted. "You look so different now from that poster picture."

"You recognized me."

"Yeah, but I've seen you for weeks—before you grew that beard. Ivester saw a guy in flannel and denim, unshaved and kinda scruffy. Sounds like eighty percent of the men round here. Thank your lucky stars he and Curtis both saw you thataway."

"Oh, for crying out loud! I'd forgotten about the FBI." He jumped up and started stuffing the few things he had in the grip.

"You might as well keep that thing packed, the way you keep leaving and staying."

"It's packed for the last time, Abit. I've got to move on."

"I know. Della and I were talking about that before she left. She has the keys to a place she's caretaking. She's coming back after dark to take you there."

"Won't nosy neighbors wonder what's going on?"

I told him city folk would think thataway, but there were no neighbors round that place. I was talking about Cleva Hall's home. She was an old friend of Della's, and I did mean old. I reckoned she was in her nineties now, living near a niece instead of her homeplace. She asked Della to look out for it—didn't want to sell because she kept telling herself she'd be able to move back someday. When you got that old, I reckoned you needed to hang onto hope any way you could.

"You'd better finish packing," I said. "They're coming back for you tonight."

Chapter 25
Della

"How did you get the old gal's name?" Alex asked, as if I'd lost my reporter skills somewhere in the back of Coburn's.

"I made up some nonsense about a policy we had when it came to putting things on the bulletin board. Back in the day I learned that if you sound official enough, people will accept just about anything."

We'd waited until dark to move Matthew to Cleva's. When we pulled up, Abit's driveway was pitch black. We got out of the Jeep, and I couldn't see two feet in front of me. Suddenly someone brushed against me. I jumped a mile.

Abit chuckled and mumbled, "Sorry." Then he introduced Alex to Matthew—I'd forgotten they'd never met. By then our eyes had adjusted, and they shook hands and nodded in that way men do. Not all warm and friendly, but sincere.

We loaded Matthew into the backseat of the Jeep, where he lay down with a blanket over him. Abit had packed a couple of boxes of food, including those ingredients I'd wondered about when he'd had his shopping spree at Coburn's. I added a cooler full of cheeses and salami and bread, plus a fresh chicken that should keep him from starving for a week or so. I almost laughed when Abit gave Matthew a burner phone he still had from one of our capers. Not that it was funny—just surreal. I was surprised it still had minutes and that Abit had found the charger. Whatever, I was glad we could stay in touch.

Abit looked kind of lonesome as we waved goodbye and headed down the driveway, though I was sure he'd soon feel relief that he no longer hosted an amnesiac with unknown intentions. I drove fast, but we made it to Cleva's without incident. Alex helped Matthew carry his food and clothing boxes inside. We promised to check in regularly.

On the way home, Alex looked over at me. "Okay, that's done, but what about Granny? Why is she leading the charge to find Matthew? And what connection does Laurel Falls have with someone so obviously *not* from around here?"

"Drug dealing has long tentacles, Alex. Even years ago I wrote stories about older people resorting, ironically, to dealing illegal drugs just to pay for their *legal* drugs."

"So now Matthew is a big-city drug dealer with a cadre of folks up here expanding his realm?"

"Could be. Could be a good guy they need to find because he knows too much."

"Well, that tells me something."

"What?"

"I need to get back to work and find out who Imogene Caruthers is."

THE NEXT DAY, I perked up when Myrtle Ledford came into Coburn's. It wasn't her regular day, and I'd been dying to ask her about Imogene Caruthers. Alex's research was good, but there was nothing like the local grapevine.

I managed to contain my impatience and asked how she was doing.

"Go ahead," Myrtle said, chuckling. "I can tell you're about to bust a gut over something,"

Ah, the freshness of mountain bluntness, though I could feel myself blush at being so transparent. "Where does Imogene Caruthers live? I need to go see her."

"Well, you'd better wear your bulletproof vest, Della. That woman shoots first and asks questions later. You'd never get onto her front porch, let alone talk to her."

"She didn't mind coming into my store."

"That's different. That's public property, in her eyes. Her place is, well, her place. So why are you all hepped up to see Imogene?" When I explained about the poster, her expression turned serious. "Why don't I go out there and ask round? Believe it or not, we're old friends. I'm one of the few people she lets into her cabin."

"What do you know about her?"

"Well, as you can imagine, she has a whole passel of young'uns and grandbabies. Most of them are no counts round here, though one child is a real good mechanic. Maybe you take your Jeep to Tommy Caruthers?"

"I've heard of him," I said just to move things along. I had more questions. Fortunately Myrtle was used to my reporterly nosiness. "Why do you think she brought this here? And claimed the sheriff had sent her?" I asked as I unrolled the poster. I felt startled all over again to see Matthew's face staring back at me. "I can't post something like this without knowing more about it. Annie is often alone in the store, and I don't want her dealing with some crazed yahoo."

"That's wise, Della. If it's someone Imogene knows, he could be a tough character, though he looks kinda nice in that picture. We don't get many men round here wearing suit coats and ties."

I couldn't let on I knew the man; besides, at this point I was more interested in why *Granny* was involved in his story. Myrtle paused and added, "You know, that reminds me. One of her daughters married up—some lawyer down in Asheville. Their only child—a spoiled brat who's probably in high school now—has been a handful. Imogene dotes on him when he comes for long visits during summer vacation. His parents are likely thrilled to get rid of him. He's gotten in some skirmishes over the years, but Imogene thinks that shows spunk."

"What kind of trouble?"

"Oh, nothing too serious. Teenage stuff, but she likes it that he's not a goody-goody, as she puts it. I guess he inherited that streak of hers—shoot first and all that."

"So you think she might be asking around for *him*? The kid?"

"Well, it sure isn't for me or Old Man Clendenin, the only two other folks I know she can tolerate."

"You said it was her daughter. What family did she marry into?" I held my breath, worried Myrtle would finally put her foot down about all my questions. She didn't.

"Oh, they're the Maguires, Raymond and Beth Maguire. Esquire, don't you know. And the kid? I think he's James or Jason or something like that. But let me go out there first to see what's up, okay? I'd hate for you to end up with a seat full of buckshot."

Chapter 26
Abit

NO SOONER HAD MATTHEW left than here came the FBI again. I shoulda known Curtis would be back, what with that poster going up all over the place.

He'd barely stopped his government issue when he jumped out. "Abit, I had to make sure you were okay. I'm ninety percent certain that guy in the homemade poster is the one living here. What are you up to? Harboring a criminal—or did he force you to give him a hideout?"

"Which question should I answer first?"

"Oh. Sorry. Where is he?"

"He's gone. And no, he didn't hold me against my will. He was just a guy who helped me with some sanding and then moved on. You know how many drifters pass through. I was as surprised as you to see his face on that poster." That was the honest truth, and I figured saying that helped me sound more believable. Curtis always said I was a lousy liar.

"I saw him, Abit, lurking around. He seemed strange. Are you all right? And where did he go?"

I sighed. "Did you hear a thing I just said? He left. I'm fine. He said he was going somewhere west of here." I knew Cleva Hall's home was in that direction. "You can search the place. I won't even make you get a warrant."

"I just might do that. I have a strong feeling you're holding back on me. I've said it before—you're a lousy liar."

"I'm gonna start calling you Thomas."

"Oh, don't start that Bible stuff with me. I was raised on it. My mama could find a biblical reference for anything and everything!"

"So could mine, only she preferred the ones for all the bad things in life. I never could figure out why she skipped over 'Love thy neighbor' or 'Be kind to one another, tenderhearted, forgiving one another.'"

That seemed to take the steam outta him. He sat back down in the driver's seat with the car door open. "I was worried about you, Abit."

"Not to mention you wanted to catch the killer of that drug dealer in the wilderness."

"Well, there is that." He gave me a sheepish smile. Not that there was anything wrong with him wanting to find the killer. That was his job. But he had been laying it on pretty thick about my wellbeing.

"That's fine, Curtis. I appreciate your concern. But trust me, Matthew is not that killer. He's just not the type."

"That's what they all say."

"Okay, Thomas," and we both grinned.

"I'm just glad you're safe."

"Me too. And why not stay a while? I've got some fine leftovers in the freezer. After supper, we talked a while, and things felt like they were getting back to normal.

Until Della called.

Chapter 27
Della

I CALLED ABIT EVEN THOUGH I might wake him. I couldn't wait to tell him Alex had found a neighborhood with a red door boasting the numerals 1247. In Asheville.

"Hi Honey, we need to go to Asheville again, only this time Matthew should join us. Are you up for another road trip?

"Uh, that's no trouble at all. Thanks for letting me know."

"What? Abit? Are you in trouble? Is someone there? That kid?"

"Not at all. Good night." He hung up.

Something was definitely wrong. I went into the office to tell Alex about it, expecting him to calm me down. Turned out he was more worried about our boy than I was.

We took his car—a black Mercedes that wouldn't show up as much as my white Jeep, though by daylight his fancy German car was decidedly more conspicuous. He'd traded up for a model that didn't make the rattly sound that used to drive me crazy. Even so, his car embarrassed me in our small community. But no one was on the roads at that time of night, and we made it to Hanging Dog in record time.

Alex parked close to the top of the drive, cut the engine, then the lights. "Stay here for now, Della. I'll go have a look." He got out and pushed his door shut, leaving it unlatched. Didn't make a sound.

I was biting my nails, expecting a long wait while Alex looked around. But he came back in a matter of minutes. Smiling.

"I saw a government issue at the top of the drive. I'm pretty sure it's FBI."

"Curtis," we both said about the same time. I let out a sigh of relief. Abit couldn't talk because he didn't want to give anything away to the FBI. I wanted to laugh *and* cry. Instead I said, "Hey, we're all dressed up with nowhere to go. When was the last time we got out at night?"

Alex looked at our clothes. "You call this dressed up?"

"Good enough for C.J.'s."

That was a notorious nightspot in Baker County, just over the Avery County line. It welcomed visitors from surrounding dry counties for beer, beer, and more beer. But they also had live music most nights, and I felt like doing something out of the ordinary.

We drove a while and eventually crossed the county line. Up ahead, I could see C.J.'s neon sign and a parking lot so full of pickups, we had to park on a grassy verge. Before Alex turned off the engine, he said, "Are you sure about this?"

I laughed. I always was the bigger risktaker, though stopping off at C.J.'s was small potatoes in that department. Besides, I could hear music playing, and I wanted to listen up close.

Inside, years of stale beer had penetrated the wooden floor and tobacco smoke clung to the walls—almost enough to put me off. But the music was loud and a little bit raunchy, and it was just what I needed to cut through the craziness of the past couple of weeks.

Alex brought two microbrews back to our table. Things had improved lately with the trend toward local brews, something they could make in the backwoods as good as—if not better than—in the city. Mine was a lager called Mule Kicker, and it lived up to its name. Alex got Surly Sadie, an IPA with enough hops and herbs to start an apothecary.

When the band took a break, we talked a while about, what else, Matthew and our investigation. Alex had easily found Imogene Caruthers' wealthy daughter and her family in Asheville and confirmed their names and the school the kid went to. He'd also pored over all kinds of pictures on Facebook and even the *Asheville Citizen-Times*.

A different band came on, a Buck Owens tribute band. Owens was one of my favorites, so I quit talking and listened a while. They were doing a good job of "Act Naturally" and "Together Again" when Alex said, "It's him."

"No, babe, Buck's dead."

"I mean the kid. Jason Maguire. Granny's grandson."

Chapter 28
Della

MYRTLE STOPPED BY THE NEXT MORNING, more upbeat than usual. She'd been out to Caruthers's place and seemed delighted with her news. Her cheeriness grated a little, only because my head was pounding. We'd stayed late at C.J.'s in order to follow the kid, who'd practically closed the place down. By then I was full of beer and my head was replaying Buck Owens' tunes like a broken record. But Myrtle's enthusiasm was contagious.

"I've never seen Imogene so happy. In fact, I doubt that happens much. But her grandson had finally come for his annual summertime visit." Myrtle stopped and looked at some notes she's taken.

I felt a wave of deep friendship for this old friend and customer. I hadn't mentioned exactly why I needed this information, and she hadn't asked; she just wanted to help me.

"So next thing I know she's calling out to him. 'Jason, Honey, there's someone I want you to meet.' That's what she said in this kinda sweet voice real different from her everyday one.

So now we know for sure his name is Jason. Anyway, I almost didn't recognize him. That boy didn't look right. He was all skinny and drawn. I'd've thought he was sick, but Imogene would've bent my ear if he had been. Maybe it's just growing pains."

"Myrtle, I can't thank you enough. This is just what we, er, I needed. Excellent news—I mean that I now know more about the Caruthers's clan."

I kept it to myself that Alex had already uncovered most of what she'd just shared. But it was good to have confirmation that Granny more than likely had been working on Jason's behalf to locate Matthew. And we hadn't known that Jason's tweaker look wasn't his usual appearance. We'd presumed he'd used as much meth as he'd sold, but now it seemed a fair bet his physical decline was a relatively new development. My money was on a guilty conscience.

Myrtle went about her shopping in a nearby aisle. I called over to her, "When was the last time you saw Jason?"

"Oh, it musta been Christmas. Wait, no, it was Easter. He looked fine then." She shook her head, unable to make sense of his rapid decline.

When I rang up her groceries, I slipped into her bag some of her favorite things—Belgian chocolates, Scottish oatcakes, bread-and-butter pickles. I'd've given her more, but I knew she'd

done this out of friendship. Too much from me
would have insulted her.

As soon as she left, I called Alex.

Chapter 29
Abit

EARLY THE NEXT DAY, after Curtis left for Charlotte, I called Della. I figured she was worried after my strange answers on the telephone. She told me about them coming here the night before, then heading over to C.J.'s, where they'd seen that Jason kid. I wanted to ask what she and Alex were doing over at C.J.'s, but then I thought I'd sound like Mama used to. It was a honkytonk, but hey, I wished I could've gone too. Instead, I'd spent my evening trying not to give anything away to the FBI.
Chapter 30
   And they'd spotted the kid. Alex had already discovered he went to Butterfield Classical School, a fancy private school in Asheville. Turned out that wasn't far from the other address he'd found at 1247 Yellowstone Road, the one with a red door. Or St. Paul's Episcopal Church, which also had a red door. Anyway, they followed the kid after he left the joint. It musta been late because I could hear Della yawn real big over the phone. And she was kinda ornery.

With so much new information at hand, Della wanted to show Matthew all three locations to see if they woke up any memories. After sunset, I snuck out to Cleva's place to get Matthew and bring him back to the farm. We needed to get an early start, and I didn't want to move him round in daylight—or get up any earlier than I had to. Man, both dogs went nuts when they saw him again, and I didn't even feel jealous.

"Do I have to wear that awful disguise?" Matthew whined when I told him the plan.

"Do you want to get caught—before we find out what's going on?"

Matthew sighed and put his arms out in front of him, wrists together like they do on TV when they're about to slap on handcuffs. It was good to see a bit of humor from the guy.

The next morning on the drive down, Della kept singing Buck Owens songs. She said she'd heard more Buck Owens than she'd bargained for. I knew how those catchy tunes and rhyming lyrics could bring on a plague of earworms. And sure enough, pretty soon they were lodged in my head too. Matthew didn't seem to notice.

I looked into the backseat and had to bite my lip not to laugh. What Matthew called "that awful disguise" really did look a sight. He still had his beard. I was halfway expecting him to have shaved it off oncet he was hidden away at Cleva's since he was always scratching at it. And he still had those fake glasses I'd given him. I did bring him a different hat. That plus the vest and a thin flannel shirt, and I couldn't imagine anyone at Butterfield or Yellowstone Road would recognize him.

WHEN WE PULLED UP at 1247 Yellowstone Road, Matthew told Della to go ahead and park in front of the house; he wasn't worried anyone would know him. It was a fine stone house sitting high atop a hill, a setting not all that different from mine—but a world of difference in square footage and price tag. The yard was like a picture postcard—green lawn trimmed within an inch of its life, bushes and flowers lining the stone steps to the red front door. All those steps reminded me of my boyhood home, though these weren't covered in slippery moss.

Matthew took off his fake glasses and looked all round. When Della asked if he wanted to get out, he just shook his head. After a long while, I asked for the hundredth time, "Any memories?"

He nodded and seemed to have more spunk about him. "Yes, I lived there. Decades. My whole life, perhaps, if that vision I had of a small boy holds true. I believe my tenancy here ran until just a few weeks ago."

I had to wonder about the yardwork while he was away. "Did you live with someone, Matthew? I mean, who's been mowing and watering? The yard looks perfect at a time when grass grows like weeds."

"That would be Charles's doing. He'd keep up the place even though I was away. He knows I'll settle up when I get back."

I felt of two minds. One, an incredible weight lifted offa me to see he'd lived in a nice house in a ritzy neighborhood. Not that rich folks didn't do criminal things, but they tended to do them behind closed doors—not duking it out over drugs in the wilderness. But two, I felt a sorrow deep in my chest after he'd said, "when I get back." There'd been a time that would've been good news, but the guy was growing on me.

Della sat quiet-like 'til she sensed Matthew was ready to leave. She cranked the car and drove to Butterfield Classical Academy. Nothing like the school I'd loved so much in Laurel Falls. I was glad I hadn't been taken outta a school like that. I would've missed the swimming pool, tennis courts, and what was likely well-stocked classrooms on the inside.

This time Matthew seemed agitated. He leaned up between us in the front seat, his arms over the seats to get a closer look. Della'd had to park on the outside of some big iron gates, and while she idled there, he started mumbling to himself. Then he pointed toward an overgrown area just to the left of the gates. "There. There. That's where. Gunshot." He buried his face in his hands. I patted his back and was surprised to see tears coming out between his fingers.

After a while, Della asked if he was okay. "Good enough." He took a big breath, blew his nose, and added, "I know this is where I was injured, but nothing more is coming to me. Let's move on. I'd like to see the church."

As we drove there, I noticed everything was within walking distance of one another—the house, school, and church. It seemed he was used to living in a closed circle, not that different from my life.

Matthew nodded when Della stopped in front of a pretty little church with a red door. A trim white sign with black letters read St. Paul's Episcopal Church. It reminded me of the one near Laurel Falls, where Father Max used to preach. That was where I first met Alex, some twenty-five year ago. I hated him at first, but back then I was as lost as Matthew was now. We sat there for the longest time while Matthew studied the church. When a slight smile cracked his face, he said he was ready to leave.

On the way outta town, Della drove by The Men's Store, but Matthew didn't have much to say about that. Maybe he ordered stuff over the phone or online, and they delivered. It didn't really matter. We had plenty of new information to work with.

As we rode along, we went over what we knew and what we'd learned. Matthew was from Asheville. He'd been a teacher in a private school, within walking distance of both his home and his church. He owned an Irish setter that he presumably walked in the neighborhood. He had some money—otherwise that Charles guy wouldn't have kept up the yard and house so nice. No one's *that* loyal. Something happened in the triangle between the three places, likely just outside the school gates, that landed Matthew in my creek with a banged up head. Jason went to school there, and that would be just too much of a coincidence for him not to be involved.

We were gaining on the truth, though we needed help tying things together. They came together all right, but not the way any of us could have imagined.

Chapter 30
Abit

"Good to see you, Old Man," Conor said as he put down his bags to hug me. I swear he'd grown over the summer, and his voice had changed.

They'd started calling me Old Man after they'd heard so much about Baldy and his Old Man back in England. I didn't like it at first—that man had caused a lot of heartache—but by now, I found it kinda funny.

Vern came up next and said, "Ditto." I got a kick outta watching his dry sense of humor develop, his timing nearabout perfect.

Then they both squeezed in for a group hug. It felt so good, I didn't want to let go. The boys didn't either, and true to my worrying nature, I felt something must be wrong. Ends up I was right. Later that evening it came out that Fiona had started dating. (Earlier when she'd dropped Conor and Vern off, she didn't even look my way.) I reckoned seeing one of your parents going out with someone else was confusing at best. I needed to be extra regular round them, though given all that'd been going on, I wasn't sure I could pull that off. Fortunately, Matthew was back at Cleva's 'til Della and Alex could make sense of all the leads we'd uncovered.

The next day was Sunday, and the boys flat out told me they weren't going to church. When Fiona still lived on the farm, she'd made them go most Sundays, and apparently with a Catholic church nearby in Asheville, they hadn't missed a service. I couldn't blame them for not wanting to go. At least not to the kind of church Mama had made me attend. When I was just a little older than them, I'd done the same. I'd put my foot down and didn't return to Jesus 'til I was older. There's a saying—that people don't leave the church because of the teachings of Jesus; they leave because they can't bear how much people in those churches go against his teachings. I couldn't agree more. Besides, I wasn't worried about my boys' mortal souls. I was proud of them for making their own way. And when the time was right, I knew if they went looking for Jesus, he'd be waiting for them.

They had a lot of settling in to do, so after a midday dinner of leftover spaghetti and meatballs, they headed to their room. As Conor went up the stairs, he said over his shoulder, "I bet things have been awfully quiet while we were away."

I nearly spit out my coffee, but managed to just nod. "Sure were, Conor," I lied. "So glad you're both back, safe and sound." And, of course, that was the truth.

Chapter 31
Della

I WATCHED AS ABIT pulled his truck around to the side of the store to park. He'd brought Matthew to the store so we could go over more questions. They used the side door. Good thing. The store was jammed.

When I got a break, I joined them and pointed to the table where I'd laid out some worksheets. Alex and I had made a grid of questions and left room for written answers. Matthew's memory was coming back in patches, and adding even small details could help trigger more.

But the morning was wild. I had to keep running back and forth between the front of the store and the back since it was Annie's day off again. Finally, I caught a break when just before noon, everyone in Laurel Falls seemed to have gone home to make their midday dinner.

Matthew was sipping a cup of black coffee, and Abit had just taken a bite out of a lemon cream doughnut from an assortment I'd picked up earlier. That seemed the perfect time to tell them about the sheriff. "So, Matthew, I need to warn you. We're looking at a number of serious crimes, and at some point I have to bring Sheriff Horne in on this before I get in trouble for withholding evidence. Especially since the FBI is leading the investigation."

"That notion no longer panics me the way it did a few weeks ago," Matthew said with an apologetic look at Abit. "As you know, I now remember my home and the school. And the church, of course. But I'm not clear on how I got tangled up with drug dealers and Jason Maguire. I can tell you, I *do* remember he was a real pain in the classroom. He had no interest in being in any of my classes—French, art, music—and acted accordingly. All I can figure is he thought his mother and father would bail him out of any predicament he got into. And they likely would. Apparently they love him, somehow, and have spoiled him rotten."

"Or they ignored him, and he's working hard to get attention." That was Abit, someone who knew all about that scenario, though he went in the opposite direction—trying too hard to curry favor with the world. But between the two paths, I suppose he'd chosen the better one.

"Matthew, just a few more questions," I said, wanting to take advantage of the lull in the store. "Did you ..."

"Hold on, Della. I apologize, but I need the restroom. I've been drinking a lot of coffee this morning. I didn't sleep well last night, and I awoke way too early."

That's when I heard the bell over the front door ring. So much for the lull. "I'll be out in a minute," I shouted, but it must have been a tourist because no one called back.

"You go on, Della," Abit said. "I can finish filling some of this stuff in for Matthew while he's ..."

Suddenly, a scrawny kid wearing a baseball cap ran into the backroom holding a two-by-four, swinging it like a baseball bat. Abit and I were so shocked it took us a minute to duck for cover. With each blow, the extra stock stored back there came crashing to the floor near where we crouched. When his cap flew off with a particularly vicious blow, I recognized Jason, powered by one drug or another.

"Now isn't that a pretty sight? I've got you right where I want you. Who wants to be the first whack-a-mole?" he snarled.

I slowly reached in my pocket and pressed a button on my phone I knew well enough not to need to look. Then I said, "Jason, you have no reason to harm us. We're on your side."

"That's not what Memaw said. She said you were snooping around and out to get me. I didn't do anything wrong."

"We know that. In fact, take a look at the papers on the table," I said. "They lay out how you were just in the wrong place at the worst time."

"Shut up. You're just trying to confuse me."

"No, she's not, Jason. We know you were acting in self-defense." That was Abit, though his voice was an octave higher than usual. Understandably so.

"What about SHUT UP don't you understand? Now get over by that cabinet. Put your hands behind your backs." He looked around for something to tie us up with, and wouldn't you know it? An all-too-handy hank of rope hung right next to the door. He grabbed that and managed to tie our wrists before pushing us to the ground so he could wrap the rope around the legs of the built-in cabinet.

"Now, let me tell you how things are going to go. I want you to hear *my* side of the story, and then I'm leaving, and no one will find me where I'm planning to go. I don't care if that stupid twat Grayson Sterling gets blamed for everything because I'll be free as a bird by then."

"Okay, sounds fair," I said. Abit swiveled his head around like I'd lost my mind. But I had a plan too. I played a hunch. "Just tell us how Grayson came upon you and that soon-to-be dead drug dealer." (I'd assumed Grayson Sterling was *our* Matthew Ruisseau.)

"He was always walking that neurotic dog of his around the school. He lived nearby, and the old fool didn't even own a car. He couldn't drive and had to ride the *bus*, of all things, when he went into town. So he walked to school and then walked his dog around the school. I mean, get a life, old timer."

I was getting over my initial wave of fear, in part because this kid was a cliché on a rampage.

I wondered if he ever had an original thought. Even his petty drug dealing was cliché, though no need to mention any of that now. He was so wasted, his crazy scheme could turn lethal if I let my natural tendency toward sarcasm set him off. Instead I asked, "So what were you and the drug dealer doing before Matth, er, uh, Grayson walked up on you?"

"Duh, what do you think? I had some customers to supply—nothing major, just something to liven up a Wednesday evening, you know?" He started pacing around the back room, and with each lap in the relatively small space, his bravado grew. "And then Gray Goose—that's what we called him because you needed a stiff drink after suffering through one of his boring lectures—shows up with that hyper dog of his."

He paused and looked around for something, then pulled a bottle of water from a case he'd knocked on the floor. I took advantage of his break to catch my breath. His hyper energy and intense soliloquy in such a small space seemed to be stealing all the oxygen from the room.

When Jason finished half the bottle, he tipped it toward me. "Thanks. I appreciate that." Strange. He sounded like he meant it. "Manny freaked out and pulled a gun and pointed it at Gray Goose. I thought he was just showing off at first, but then he pointed it at me. Figured I'd set him up. I saw him pull back on the trigger, and it was my turn to freak. You can't imagine how that feels."

Actually I could. More times than I cared to remember, especially while living in D.C. But now was no time to swap gunpoint stories.

"I grabbed his hand, but he was stronger than me," Jason went on. "We wrestled, and the revolver fired. I thought I'd been shot because I had a terrible pain in my gut, but then I realized that was from the punch he gave me with his other hand. I'm not sure what happened next. I was so mixed up, but happy my guts weren't the ones blown open. That was when Sterling came over to check on me. At the time—I was confused, remember—I thought he wanted to hurt me too. I pushed him hard away from me, and his head struck one of those big blocks of granite that support the iron fence around the school. If that isn't a metaphor for what it's like at that school, I don't know what is. Anyway, I thought Sterling was dead—he was out cold. Just that dog jumping around going crazy. I gave Rover some Xanax, and he eventually went out too."

Jason took a deep breath, looking spent from all the drugs and drama. Some of what he told us answered lingering questions, but some of it seemed self-serving. Even so, more than likely the scenario spoke of self-defense and a terrible accident. If he'd turned himself in at that time, he would have gotten off with little to no detention. But he compounded everything by dumping bodies and hiding out. He looked scared and lost, which told me he did have a conscience under all that gangster persona.

He finished the bottle of water, which seemed to revive him and began strutting around the backroom. Then he kicked poor Abit in the thigh. "I don't like the way you've been looking at me, big boy. I want to teach you a lesson. Now where's that two-by-four?"

"Wait, Jason. You've had a horrible ordeal. I think I can help you," I said, trying anything to stall for time.

"You're just saying that, playing nice to try to dupe me. My dad says people do that all the time."

I ignored him, biting back a snarky lawyer comment perched on the tip of my tongue. "You must have been so scared. Is that when you moved the bodies up to Avery County?"

"Hey, you're not so stupid after all. Yeah, that's exactly what I did. And it worked until that hiker found Manny. But no one found Gray Goose, so I drove up and went to where I'd dumped him and his blamed dog. He wasn't there. I double-checked, and I knew I was at the right parking lot. I hiked all around, but no sign of him. At first I was happy he wasn't dead, but then it struck me that he could identify me. That was when I made the poster and got Memaw to help find him. But I haven't. So I'm planning to make a run for it."

Jason reached for another bottle of water. I struggled against the ropes, but got nowhere. When he turned his back to us, I tried to kick out at him. Abit joined me, but we were useless.

Then suddenly, Jason dropped to his knees before falling face first on the floor.

Everything stopped—no sound, no movement, no cogent thoughts. Just silence. It took a moment before I saw what had happened. A good-size rock had somehow connected with the back of his head. I doubted he was seriously harmed, just out for the count.

I looked around and saw Matthew standing by the restroom door. I'd forgotten all about him in the flurry of insults and information spewing from Jason. Not wasting a moment, Matthew ran over and pulled something from his vest pockets: a red bandana he tied across Jason's mouth and behind his head and some sturdy wire he crafted into makeshift handcuffs.

Matthew released us from our rope restraints. Just as we were standing, I heard the front door crash open. I ran to the front, where Sheriff Horne stood with a battering ram. Apparently Jason had locked the front door behind him. One of Horne's deputies stepped around him, pointing a gun dangerously close to me.

"You're safe now, Della," Horne said in his trademark booming voice.

"No disrespect meant, but I was safe before you got here, thanks to Matthew. Er, Matthew?" I looked all around, but he and Abit were gone.

Chapter 32
Abit

I DROVE OFF LIKE a madman, tires squealing as I banked a sharp turn. Before long, though, my nerves gave out, and I couldn't keep the steering wheel steady. I pulled over at a layby, put the truck in park, and for the first time looked over at Matthew. He was doing a lot better than me. In fact, I reckoned he was feeling proud of himself.

"Thanks for saving my life, Matthew."

"Ha! What was that you said a few weeks ago? Don't make it out to be so heroic, or some such thing. To be honest, putting up with years of surly teenagers powered that flying rock as much as wanting to help you and Della."

"That vest sure came in handy," I said, "but why were you walking round with rocks in your pockets?" I could still see two or three lumps poking outta his pockets.

"I'd found them on my walk early this morning—dark gray ones and a rusty red, each with white lines running all around them. Beautiful in the morning fog. I was struck by how the quartz—or is it calcite?—made those undulating white lines along the outer edges. I remember Dr. Robson, the geology teacher at school, talking about them. I believe that's why they caught my eye. When I picked them up, I recalled a legend he'd shared about them being wishing stones, though he was too much of a scientist to believe in that. But this morning, I figured what did I have to lose? I picked them up and wished all good things would come to you."

"Me? Why didn't you wish you'd get your memory back? Or that you'd get to go home?"

He smiled. "Believe me, I would have, but that legend includes a warning that you have to wish for someone else. I figured you wanted to get rid of me, so if I wished good things for you, I'd likely get what I wanted too."

I wasn't sure I felt the way he'd said, but I had to chuckle at his logic. "Okay, but how did you get to be such a good shot?"

"Oh, dear. This is all coming back to me now, and it's rather embarrassing. Truth be known, I'm a crack lacrosse player. Some of the faculty get together to play at the school, which has a beautiful lacrosse field. Of course, we use sticks rather than free throwing."

There was no *of course* about it for me, and I told him so. He explained that lacrosse sticks looked like sturdy butterfly nets, and they used those to fling the ball into the other team's goal. "I remember it as mostly a rich kids' game, but I like the exercise," Matthew said. "And it developed my muscles so I could fling that rock at Jason with strength and accuracy."

I asked him more questions, but there were still some gaps in his memory. Maybe with time, he'd get back to being a full Matthew. Or was it Grayson?

WHEN WE GOT TO the farm, the phone was ringing off the hook. Seemed Matthew and I needed to return to the store right away. Sheriff Horne and Curtis Maynard were mad we'd left, but I'd just wanted to get us as far away from all that craziness as I could. I'd had a summer of it, and I was sick of living thataway.

By the time we walked back into Coburn's, Jason was singing like a meadowlark. First off, he'd thrown the dealer's gun into the French Broad River in Asheville. Not much chance of finding it, though they'd sent down divers. And something I'd wondered about got answered—why no one put out a missing person report on Matthew. Jason had stolen Matthew's ID and phone, texted the school that he (Matthew) was fed up and quit, which is why no one gave his absence a second thought. His family home was long ago paid for, so no bank came calling for mortgage payments, and utilities were taken care of with automatic payments. Not that he was gone all that long—just a little over a month, so nothing seemed off to anyone. Put another way, no one had missed him. I recalled with an ache in my chest what he'd said about his cooking—that he worried he'd done a lot of it, but just for himself. Alone.

Chapter 33
Della

I RETURNED TO DUTY at Coburn's, which felt like a breeze after dealing with Jason and Matthew/Grayson. I hoped I'd never grumble about being bored at the store again. Even the constant complainers seemed kind of quaint, at least for now.

When Jason had first accosted us in the backroom, Alex had answered my silent call. But I'd forgotten he wasn't upstairs; he was driving to Chapel Hill for a meeting. He called Sheriff Horne and 911 and turned his car around, pulling up just as Horne made his grand entrance.

Later that afternoon, we were both in the backroom, clearing the mess Jason had made. Horne just stood around watching. After his deputy transported Jason to the jail in Newland, he had the nerve to ask me why I hadn't kept him better informed.

"You've got to be kidding me, Mr. I Can't Be Bothered," I'd said.

"Well, if you'd told me more about this situation, I would have been able to help."

"Oh, okay, now I've got it."

"Got what?"

"Why your last name is Horne."

"Because that was my daddy's name?"

Alex stepped over to try to calm me before I crossed a line. Too late. "No, because you sit on your butt and then try to *horn* in on the glory." Horne looked so hurt I grabbed a couple of the doughnuts from the table. "Here. Now get out of my store."

After Abit and Matthew returned to Coburn's, we all faced a grilling from Curtis Maynard. I'd closed up the store best I could with plywood—the door would need to be replaced—and posted a note saying sorry but Coburn's was closed for the day. No need to explain. By then the grapevine had informed everyone, though its accuracy was always questionable.

We were all sitting in the back room. Curtis lectured Abit about his driving away, but he didn't really seem too concerned about that breach of procedure. He took Abit's and Matthew's statements and let them go. Then he took mine and left for the Charlotte Field Office.

The next day, I got a pleasant surprise (for a change) when my old Fourth Estate friend and colleague, Jessie Walsh, rode in from D.C. to cover the story for the *Washington Post*. It was big enough news to pique her editor's interest, and she'd grown up here and knew many of the players. When she'd worked for the *Mountain*

Weekly, we'd collaborated on a couple of stories that involved Laurel Falls, one that earned her the job at the Post. I was pleased to see her rise in status hadn't gone to her head. She was as friendly and professional as ever.

As things turned out for Jason, Raymond Maguire worked a deal to get his son a short detention followed by community service. Never mind Jason had sold a bunch of meth to kids and dumped a couple of bodies. All that was difficult to prove by the time his father was through reshaping the story. Besides, Jason was still a juvenile, and a sympathetic judge chalked it up to his being a scared kid. Maybe.

People like that have a way of ruining things for others. When I think of the hard life Abit lived when he was Jason's age, and how he managed against all odds to turn out so well, I couldn't help but rage against the inequalities of life. Too often arrogance and money win out. But then I thought of Abit's life—two fine boys, a thriving woodworking business, his bluegrass band, a farm as pretty as you please—and I knew he possessed things more glorious than Jason could ever buy.

Chapter 34
Abit

WHEN THE COPS ALL WENT AWAY and Jason was out of our lives, Matthew asked if he could stay on a few weeks. He wanted to rest and experience fall foliage up close. He'd seen it in Asheville all his life, he said, but that looked more like a picture postcard—from a distance. He wanted to be *in* its amazing glory, and I couldn't blame him. All those oranges and reds and yellows stretching clear across to the horizon were a spectacle to behold, even for me after forty year.

That was the easy part. The hard part was trying to talk him out of moving back to his old life in Asheville. He said he felt the need to pick up the pieces. After all, he'd lived that life for more than fifty year and this one for only a few months. He had a point.

I kept trying, though. He'd become a friend, and the boys liked him too. He'd already taught Vern some cooking tricks, and we were all enjoying his fancy piccatas and frittatas. I thought about how much I'd worried early on that he'd act out and scare the boys. Now we were all going to miss him. That should be a lesson to me. Maybe someday I'd learn not to worry so much, especially since mostly those fears never came to pass. Some awful stuff I never saw coming may come raining down on me, but not from my worries.

Matthew seemed like a different person now that the pressures were off and he could just be himself. I could tell he still had trouble knowing whether he was Grayson Sterling or Matthew Ruisseau, but only he could work through that. "For now, I guess I'm both," he told us one evening over supper.

While Matthew and I had hung out on the farm—like when we'd been sitting round watching summer lightning or cooking hot dogs over the fire—he'd often said he'd like to live in such a peaceful place. So I figured why not help him with that?

One evening, after the boys had gone to bed, I offered to sell him a piece of my land—a coupla acres that sloped down to the creek with a spectacular view of the Black Mountains. That seemed a fitting parcel, all things considered.

He looked surprised. "Are you sure you want to bifurcate your land?"

"No, I'm not at all sure I want to *bifurcate* it, but I want to sell you a coupla acres. You won't find a prettier place. We could walk down there tomorrow, and I can show you. I used to dream of building an underground house there." He made a face. "I know what you mean. That's how I felt when I first heard about living underground, but it's not all dark with roots dangling down." I chuckled remembering that's what I'd first pictured. "They have lots of light, and the best part is they're warm in the winter and cool in the summer." I showed him some plans I'd drawn up along with a coupla magazine articles I'd saved.

He studied them a while and nodded. "That's amazing, Abit. And you're right. Those homes are lovely. Filled with light. So why don't *you* build your dream house there?"

"I've got only the two boys now, and they'll be leaving here before I could get it finished. I'd need a good number of years to finance and build it. But you could start tomorrow!"

Turned out Matthew did come from money, but I wasn't suggesting he buy that land so I could make a profit. I was offering because he seemed too good of a friend to let go. We were both private types, but we'd come to know each other without the need for a lot of words. We'd traveled our paths to find out who we were, and now we were both finally free enough to make our own choices. And in that way, we'd become brothers, of a sort.

I carried on with a few more benefits like a good spring for his water and perfect southern exposure for solar so he could be off the grid, if he wanted. He thanked me and said he'd sleep on it.

We left it at that and said good night.

IN THE END, MATTHEW decided to go back to being Grayson Sterling. "I'd love to stay up here," he told me a few days before leaving, "but my home of five decades is calling to me. I will never forget your kindness, Abit. I know it's the basis for your religion, but I think you've exceeded even that lofty goal. What we have is friendship, and that goes deeper than kindness. The way I see it, friendship is like kindness dressed in diamonds. Thank you for giving me that." I couldn't speak, just stood there with a big lump in my throat. He went on. "Oh, and I plan to take driving lessons so I can come visit, if you'll have me in your barn."

I couldn't help myself. "What about that marquetry project you started? It looks really good. You need to finish it." I was about to bring up some other things he should stick round for, but his pitying look stopped me. I knew he had a house and a church to return to. Then I recalled something else. "Remember a while ago when we talked about maybe good, maybe bad?"

"I do, and I think you ticked me off at the time."

"Oh, you were just having one of your ups and downs that day. But this so-called bad experience we've shared, it's brought a lot of good. I don't know how or why, but you coming here, at this time, means something, Matthew.

I want to hold onto that, not just let it be one more thing that passes through my life."

He thanked me, but stood to go finish packing.

THE DAY HE LEFT, the morning broke bright and warm. That felt like a stick in my eye. I knew it woulda been harder to load everything if a storm had come through, but that woulda seemed more fitting. Then again, Matthew didn't have much to move. That left plenty of room in the back of the truck for Red, tucked into a big crate; I put a blanket over it to keep the wind from scaring him. Mollie watched with a worried look. When I couldn't think of anything else to delay our leaving, I hopped into the driver's seat. I cranked the engine and looked in the rearview mirror at the boys waving until we could no longer see one another.

Matthew and I didn't have much to say on the drive down, though it was a comfortable silence. When we got to his home, he gave me a tour of the house and gardens, but my heart wasn't in it. All I could think was Asheville kept taking everything that mattered to me.

I carried his things into his house. They were light compared to the heaviness I felt on the drive home.

The boys were waiting supper for me, even though it was getting late. Vern had made biscuits and vegetable soup, and I don't know when anything tasted better. I hugged them both, and we managed to play a little music before bed. It wasn't much past nine o'clock when we all said goodnight after a long, hard day.

Chapter 35
Abit

March 2010

IT TOOK TIME, BUT things got back to normal. A few month ago, I put an ad in the newspaper and hired a new assistant in my woodshop. And if you can believe it, his name was Jason. Not that one, but the coincidence gave me a shiver. He was the most qualified, or I might've skipped over him.

I was back to playing regular-like with the Rollin' Ramblers. Felt good, and my mando sounded better than ever, though I kept worrying about Fiona taking it away. To be on the safe side, I'd sent off for some plans. I figured someday I'd make one just the way I wanted.

And I'd learned something important about myself. I *did* have friends. More than I thought. I chuckled recalling the parade up and down my drive, upsetting Matthew and making me wonder who was next. And Annie Totherow had been stopping by too. Those friends coming round reminded me how Matthew had told me to quit running my old script, as he'd called it. He was right—and I was making headway with my new one.

True to his word, Matthew (I was still having trouble calling him Grayson) kept in touch. He'd passed his driving test and came for a visit round Christmas last year. He'd bought himself a four-wheel drive SUV, though I couldn't imagine why he needed a utility vehicle in Asheville. Me and the boys loved seeing him—and Mollie was thrilled to have Red back for a spell.

Matthew had kept in touch since then with some newsy letters—I told him I was gonna nickname him the News Bee—about what he was up to in Asheville. I'd spend half the time reading and the other half looking up big words, which always made me smile. To be honest, it didn't sound like he was doing all that much, but that wasn't for me to say.

One evening when I was alone on the farm, just sitting round drinking beer by the fire, Mollie by my side, the phone rang. I didn't get many calls that time of night. I answered quickly, worried the boys might be sick or in trouble down in Asheville.

Without so much as a hello, I heard Matthew ask, "Does that offer still stand?"

My answer came easy. "'Til the cows come home."

Read an excerpt from the next book in the series, *Unwrapped*, following a note from the author.

YOUR FREE BOOK IS WAITING FOR YOU

Free prequel novelette!

Spend more time with Abit & Della

Learn how Della & Abit met

Takes place 1981-1984

VISIT
https://BookHip.com/CGPGFA
FOR YOUR FREE COPY

OR CLICK <u>HERE</u> TO GET YOUR FREE COPY

Dear Readers ...

I hope you enjoyed this book in my Appalachian Mountain Mysteries series. I sure enjoy writing them! I've been a professional writer for several decades now (I got my start in the mountains of N.C.), and it still thrills me when readers write to me. Sometimes they have questions about the stories and the characters. Other times they leave reviews and, well, make my day!

> "Reminds me of *To Kill a Mockingbird* ... finding your books is like finding a rare jewel." ~J.M. Grayson

> "After reading the first book, I read all the others as quickly as possible!" ~ Ruth H.

I'd really appreciate it if you'd take a minute to leave a review. (It's easy—just a sentence or two is enough.) Reader reviews are the lifeblood of any author's career. In today's online world, they can make a huge difference—so thanks in advance.

These days, I spend my time writing my Appalachian Mountain Mysteries series. I started them as a way to share amazing stories from my back-to-the-land experience in the N.C. mountains. I made mistakes by the wheelbarrow load, but I wouldn't take anything for those years.

I get a kick out of hearing from readers, so don't be a stranger! I'd love to hear your thoughts about Abit Bradshaw, Della Kincaid, and the whole Laurel Falls gang. Write me at lyndabooks@pm.me .

Happy reading!
Lynda McDaniel

P.S. I thought you might enjoy an excerpt from the next book in the series after the Book Club Discussion Guide.

P.P.S. And I hope you'll take advantage of my offer for a free subscription to **Spellbound Mystery Magazine**. Weekly issues are packed with fun facts and book recommendations that make finding a good book easy! Learn more at https://spellboundmysterywriters.substack.com/

Excerpt Book 7
Unwrapped

Laurel Falls, N.C.
Autumn 2012

"Della," I said in a half-whisper. "I'm reading a book about a girl who may have been killed."

I'd asked Della Kincaid to step into the kitchen so we could talk private. She and her ex-husband/boyfriend, Alex Covington, had joined me and my two boys for supper, the same day as I'd uncovered the girl's story.

"Well, if it's a good mystery, let me read it next."

"No, I mean it's a diary, in the girl's own hand."

Della went quiet. I could tell she was turning over what I'd just said. "What did she write that makes you think she came to harm?"

"She told the saddest stories and then just stopped."

"Teenagers and their diaries—they can start and stop on a whim."

"Mid-sentence?"

"Oh. Maybe you'd better start at the beginning."

Chapter 1: Abit

"Lost: One Chuh-hooa-hooa."

It took us a minute, but then my boy, Conor, and I started laughing our heads off. We had to explain to Vern, my younger boy, that the radio announcer was talking about a Chihuahua dog. You couldn't blame the announcer. Sure, those dogs are as common round here as varmints (and in my opinion, the little ankle-biters *are* varmints), but if you'd never seen that name spelled out, you'd likely pronounce it thataway.

Not long after, though, a wave of shame came over me for making fun like that—especially me, given the way I'd struggled early on at school. That was how I'd gotten my name—Daddy told everyone I was "a bit slow," and well, Abit just stuck. Turned out he was wrong on so many counts, but still, I'd suffered under that curse and shouldn't've made fun of someone else's mistakes. Of course our laughter was miles away and that airwave had already drifted off like a finger of fog in the sun. Besides, you had to laugh at life whenever you could. Some sadness or other was just lying in wait, fixing to strike.

Our being together on a Saturday morning wasn't all that common anymore. The boys were growing up and enjoyed time with their friends. But this day, we were all home, listening to the local station's Swap Shop program. It was kinda old-timey, but I was glad they hadn't done away with the show. A nice mix of local news, want ads, and for-sale items. I got up to pour more coffee when I heard Conor say, "Daddy, come quick."

Jeb Samson (not the one we'd been laughing at; that was likely his boy) was carrying on about a walnut dresser for sale. Conor had been asking me to make him a dresser for the better part of a year, but like the cobbler's son going barefoot, he was still using an old bookshelf for his clothes. I worked hard to keep food on the table with my furniture-making, and there always seemed to be some project I needed to finish for a paying customer. It had become a sore point between us.

I got back to the living room in time to hear, "Four drawers and in really good condition. The owner said his mama got it when she set up her married home. I'm sad to report he's clearing out the family homeplace after both his parents have passed." Jeb paused a moment outta respect. "Now this fine dresser won't be on the auction block for long. I know you can't see it on the radio, but if you've come to trust me over the years, take my word for it. This is a find."

When I looked round for my phone, Conor was holding his out, already dialed to the number Jeb kept barking at us. Conor had put the phone on speaker so he and Vern could listen to the bidding. I went up against two others, but I was determined to win. When the boys heard the announcer say Abit Bradshaw in Hanging Dog was the proud new owner, they both slapped me on the back and let out a little cheer.

Later, after I'd dropped them off at their school where a soccer game had already started, I headed over to the radio station. Jeb's truck was parked out front. Everybody knew it—the painting on the side said it all: "Samson's Septic. We're #1 in the #2 Business." The Swap Shop job was just a sideline; nearabout everyone round here worked at least two jobs.

Jeb was waiting for me at the door with a big smile. I soon sensed it as part friendly and part con artist. I'd gotten so caught up in the auction that I hadn't considered that "this fine dresser" might not be so fine after all. I looked down where Jeb had set it on the driveway and saw plenty of hours of refinishing ahead. I didn't say anything when I paid up, but I could tell Jeb was mighty pleased with himself—and the cut he'd take.

Didn't matter. Conor was happy, for a change. I planned to set to work on it as soon as I got home. I tried to show both boys how much they meant to me, even if this time it was for Conor.

Not that Vern was the kinda boy who needed everything to be tit for tat. He knew he got fair and square. Besides, envy wasn't in his makeup. He'd had a rough upbringing before he came to live with us, and I reckoned he'd never forgotten how much his luck had changed.

I knew it wasn't really the dresser that had Conor acting out. Both the boys were kinda shook up over the fact that their mother and my ex-wife, Fiona, had remarried. Sure, the fellow sounded nice enough, but still, I could tell they were uneasy with yet another change in their young lives. And it'd torn clear through me when I'd overheard Vern saying to Conor how that meant we'd never get back together again. Of course I already knew that, but young'uns' hearts are still open to hope.

I pulled up next to my woodworking shop and unloaded the dresser under a maple tree where I liked to work, what with shade in the summer and full sun come winter. The weather had already begun its slide into winter, green leaves leaning into gold and red, some already turning brown. But today carried a warmth broken only by the occasional soft breeze. As I scrubbed off layers of dirt from the dresser, a phoebe told me its name over and over, and a pair of purple martins swooped round the gourds I'd hung for them in nearby trees. They'd be leaving soon for warmer climes, so I took a moment to enjoy their cavorting with the drifting leaves.

I turned back to my work without regret. I liked refinishing almost as much as making something new. The old furniture had a story to tell about the people who'd owned it. Too much polish said one thing. Messages carved in the wood told anothern. Tobacco and wood smoke smothered fine wood, leaving it dried out and neglected, like some folks' lives.

This piece, though, was made from a rich walnut that shone through as I gave it a good cleaning. In the corner of my eye, I could see a squirrel kinda tiptoe my way. Maybe the smell of fresh walnut wood made him think there were nuts nearby. He'd been poking round for a couple year now, though I hadn't seen him lately, stirring worries he'd made his way into someone's Brunswick stew. I'd named him Sparky because of a burned area, hairless and scorched, on his back, likely from some kinda fire, maybe electrical. He sat on his hind legs and chattered at me, not happy to discover I had nothing close at hand for him to eat. "Go over to the birdfeeder, Sparky, and gorge yourself like you usually do," I scolded right back.

"Talking to yourself now, are you?" Matthew said, a big grin on his face.

I had one too when I answered. "Not just *now*. For a long time. It's the only way I can say something without irritating someone, though sometimes I even annoy myself."

Matthew was neighbor and friend, more like brother. Last year he'd moved onto some land I'd sold him, where he built a striking underground house. I'd thought he was growing to love it here following a lifetime in Asheville with all its noise and nonsense, but after a time, oncet his home project was done, he grew restless. He missed teaching, he told me one night as we sat drinking beer by the fire.

I had to hand it to him. This area wasn't known for good jobs, but he'd found himself a teaching position just south of Boone. Not at my old school, The Hickson School of American Studies (aka The Hicks), but some fancy one for rich kids. He was used to dealing with that kinda situation and seemed happy there. But with a thirty-minute commute on good days (way longer during leaf-peeping season), we didn't see enough of each other.

Matthew had been my woodworking assistant while he recovered from an injury, so he spotted the gently figured grain and quality workmanship that became obvious the more I rescued the dresser from neglect. All I could figure was the previous owner had stored it on a porch or in a barn oncet she no longer had a place for it in her house.

"Those are some fine joints," he said, pouring coffee from the electric percolator I'd recently bought for the shop. "And I like your new coffeepot. This is a good addition."

I had to laugh. Back when we'd worked together, we'd both taken plenty of breaks to go to the house for coffee. More to get a little fresh air and some alone time (close quarters in my shop) than to drink more caffeine, which only gave us the jitters. Not smart round power tools.

"In spite of some mistreatment, that dresser looks like something of value," he added.

I took out the top drawer to study the dovetail joints closer. Almost as good as those made by Shiloh, born Bob Greene, who'd worked with me before Matthew. When Matthew left to teach again, I hired a guy named Jason—but I had to let him go last month. He turned the air blue with all his swearing. Thing was, the fellow was as nice and friendly as you please, but when he was working, he'd start cussing and carrying on. At first I thought he'd hurt himself, and I'd drop what I was doing to tend to him. He'd act surprised, like he was wondering what was wrong with *me*. He musta gone into some kinda trance while he worked and became a different person. It was sorta funny at first, such a mild-mannered person acting thataway, but after a while, it wore on me. So it had been just me for a coupla months, which was why I was so behind with my orders.

"Yep, I think this will polish up real smart. Conor should be pleased."

"Is he getting any better?"

Matthew knew about Conor being all angry about his mother, his father, life in general. A teenager. "A little," I said after a lengthy pause. "We're all working through some stuff right now."

He raised his eyebrows, but then looked at his watch. "Sorry, but I need to get a move on."

He was kinda cagey thataway. I think he might've had a date. Some folks did stuff like that on a Saturday night. I sighed, thinking how mine had turned so quiet—unless our bluegrass band, the Rollin' Ramblers, had a gig. Then Annie Totherow came to mind. I'd known her for a long time—all but five year of my life. Her daddy was a beekeeper, and when I was still a boy, I helped Della pick up cases of his famed sourwood honey for Coburn's General Store. I still remember visiting Annie's house and passing by her room, all pink and pretty. Smelling nice too.

I turned back to the dresser and got two more drawers out, but I had to fight with the middle one. It seemed caught on the frame and came out only halfway. I pulled hard, but that dang thing wouldn't budge. I figured the bottom had drooped, though when I looked inside the drawer, the part I could see appeared to be level with the sides. Same thing when I turned it over.

Looking back, I wondered how different life would've been if I'd left that drawer alone. It, or rather what was inside, turned everything upside down.

Unwrapped is available at most online book retailers, as are all the other books in the Appalachian Mountain Mysteries series.

Lynda McDaniel Books

FICTION
Waiting for You
A Life for a Life(permafree)
The Roads to Damascus
Welcome the Little Children
Murder Ballad Blues
Deep in the Forest
Up the Creek
Unwrapped
After Dusk
Deep South Trouble
Appalachian Mountain Mysteries Box Set
A Life for a Life Audiobook

NONFICTION
Words at Work (permafree)
How Not to Sound Stupid When You Write
How to Write Stories that Sell
Write Faster Series Box Set

www.ingramcontent.com/pod-product-compliance
Lightning Source LLC
Chambersburg PA
CBHW050841180626
46814CB00007B/2562